D0639352

DOUBLE FEATURE

Also by Maggie Dana

Keeping Secrets, Timber Ridge Riders (Book 1)
Racing into Trouble, Timber Ridge Riders (Book 2)
Riding for the Stars, Timber Ridge Riders (Book 3)
Wish Upon a Horse, Timber Ridge Riders (Book 4)
Chasing Dreams, Timber Ridge Riders (Book 5)
Almost Perfect, Timber Ridge Riders (Book 6)
Taking Chances, Timber Ridge Riders (Book 7)
After the Storm, Timber Ridge Riders (Book 8)

The Golden Horse of Willow Farm, Weekly Reader Books
Remember the Moonlight, Weekly Reader Books
Best Friends series, Troll Books

TIMBER RIDGE RIDERS
∽ Book Nine ∾

James L. Hamner Public Library
Amelia Court House, VA 20002

DOUBLE
FEATURE

Maggie Dana

899

Amazon

1-2016

933529

PAGEWORKS PRESS

Double Feature © 2014 Maggie Dana
www.maggiedana.com

All rights reserved. Except as permitted under the U.S. Copyright
Act of 1976, no part of this publication may be reproduced,
distributed, or transmitted in any form or by any means, or
stored in a database or retrieval system, without prior written
permission of the publisher.

This is a work of fiction. While references may be made to actual
places or events, all names, characters, incidents, and locations
are from the author's imagination and do not resemble any
actual living or dead persons, businesses, or events.
Any similarity is coincidental.

ISBN 978-0-9851504-8-8

Edited by Judith Cardanha
Cover by Margaret Sunter
Interior design by Anne Honeywood
Published by Pageworks Press
Text set in Sabon

for Kathy, Tim, and Sarah

1

HOLLY CHAPMAN COUNTED STRIDES as her horse approached the last jump. "One, two, three . . . and up." Magician launched himself forward, tucked his front legs, and popped the double oxer like a kangaroo.

Mom wasn't going to like it.

But at least they'd jumped clear. Slowing down, Holly patted Magician's sweaty neck and kicked both feet free of her stirrups. Their lesson was almost over, thank goodness, because her legs had just about had enough. Jennifer West pulled her horse, Rebel, away from the others and rode up to Holly.

"You busy later?" she said.

Holly shrugged. "No."

Apart from cleaning tack and mucking stalls, the rest of Holly's day yawned empty and miserable—just like yesterday and the one before that—all the way back to that awful, horrible day when her best friend, Kate Mc-Gregor, had left the barn. She'd only been gone for two weeks but already it felt like two months.

"Cool," Jennifer said in a stage whisper. "Meet us in the tack room." She glanced toward the far end of the indoor where Angela Dean and Kristina James were giggling and paying no attention to Holly's mother, the riding team's instructor.

"*Us?*" Holly said, following Jennifer's gaze.

"No, silly. Not them."

Jennifer held a finger to her lips, then pulled off her gloves, and re-tied the glittery green bow on Rebel's mane. It matched the shamrock stickers plastered all over Jennifer's orange vest and the tufts of green hair that stuck out from beneath her helmet.

Two weeks ago Jennifer's hair had been red for Valentine's Day. At Easter, Holly predicted, it would be bright yellow and her riding helmet would sprout bunny ears.

"Then, who?" Holly said.

"Me, Sue, and Robin."

"Okay, sure. But what's all the mystery about?"

"Getting Kate back to Timber Ridge."

It's what Holly wanted, too—more than anything. With a sigh, she yanked off her helmet and shook out her blond pony tail. "Good luck," she said, trying not to sound morose. "But it won't work. Robin and Sue are still mad at her."

They'd once cheered Kate at horse shows, taught her to ski, and hung out with her after school. But when Kate and Holly had a really dumb fight, the barn's friendships had unraveled and kids had taken sides.

"They've gotten over it," Jennifer said.

"Really?"

"Yes, really," Jennifer said. "But don't tell Liz about us getting together."

"Mom's got eyes in the back of her head. She—"

"She won't be here," Jennifer said, pocketing her cell phone. "My mother just texted. Mrs. Dean's called another committee meeting."

"Now?"

"Like, immediately," Jennifer said.

Holly groaned. "What is it *this* time?"

Angela's mother was the self-appointed Queen Bee of Timber Ridge. She ruled the Homeowners' Association with an iron fist, meddled constantly in barn affairs, and blamed Mom if Angela didn't win blue ribbons.

"Dunno," Jennifer said, grinning. "Tablecloths for the Timber Ridge hospitality tent at the Festival of Horses?"

"But that's not until April," Holly said.

Not that she'd be competing. Magician had pulled up lame right before the first qualifying show in December, so Holly had ridden Kate's horse, Tapestry. Then, at the next show, Kate had ridden Magician. They'd both qualified for the finals in April on each other's horses, along with Jennifer on Rebel and Angela with her expensive new warmblood, Ragtime.

The Festival of Horses was a hugely important show.

Scouts from the United States Equestrian Federation would be there looking for junior talent. But the show rules firmly stated that you had to ride the horse you qualified on.

Except that Tapestry and Kate had left the barn.

They were no longer part of the Timber Ridge team which meant Holly couldn't ride at all unless Mom managed to convince the show officials to let her ride Magician instead.

So far, no luck.

"Listen up, girls," Liz called out. "Lesson's not over yet. I want a sitting trot, no stirrups, twice around the arena." She paused. "Then I want you to do a posting trot."

"Without our stirrups?" Angela said.

"Yes," replied Liz.

"No way," Angela snapped, digging both heels into Ragtime. Her startled horse bolted forward, almost unseating his rider as they catapulted toward the arena door. Kristina hesitated, then kicked her palomino into a trot and followed Angela into the barn.

There was an embarrassed silence.

Jennifer coughed, Sue looked the other way, and Holly crammed her helmet back on. Poor Mom. It was a no-win situation. If she pushed Angela to work harder, Angela complained to her mother. But if Angela didn't win blue ribbons, Mrs. Dean complained to Mom.

* * *

For the third time in as many minutes, Kate McGregor checked her iPhone. Ten o'clock on Friday morning—last day of winter break. The others would be having a riding lesson at Timber Ridge, and Kate wasn't included.

Rubbing soap into Tapestry's already clean saddle, Kate glanced around their new home. Despite the frigid temperatures outside, Mr. Evans's tiny tack room was warm and cozy. A jug of hot cider sat on a wooden trunk, one of Aunt Bea's knitted afghans lay across a red leather chair, and a stack of horse magazines waited for those moments when Kate ran out of things to do.

Like right now.

So far she'd cleaned both stalls, raked down the aisle, and swept the feed room. Then she'd made sure the barn's red-handled brooms, pitchforks, and shovels were hung up neatly the way Mr. Evans liked.

There wasn't a cobweb in sight.

Woodwork gleamed, brass hinges shone, and all the buckets were stacked up like a kid's sorting toy. Max, the barn's inscrutable red tabby, sat washing his paws on top of a black wheelbarrow that Kate had just scrubbed. It was so clean that it looked as if nobody ever used it.

Through the open door Kate caught a glimpse of Mr. Evans's chestnut gelding, Pardner. A white blaze covered most of Pardner's homely face, and Kate hardly noticed his mismatched eyes any more. In the stall beside him, Tapestry gave a soft whicker.

Standing up, Kate reached into her pocket for two large carrots—one for each horse. Tapestry stretched out her copper-colored nose and whickered even louder. Then Pardner joined in.

As Kate was feeding them, the barn door opened and Mr. Evans walked toward her. "You spoiling those horses again?"

"Look who's talking," Kate said, grinning.

Mr. Evans carried a small red colander filled with apple cores and peelings that he shared between Pardner and Tapestry. "Aunt Bea made another pie yesterday," he said. "So you best come into the kitchen when you're done out here, or it'll all be gone."

Mr. Evans wasn't wearing his cowboy hat, and Kate tried hard not to stare at the splotchy red birthmark that covered half his cheek, then curved around one ear, and spread across his shiny bald head like a map of Indonesia.

"You can look," he said. "I don't mind."

"I know," Kate said, blushing.

She hated being caught staring like she had been two weeks ago in the village. It was the first time she'd seen Mr. Evans without his hat, and he'd just offered her a stall for Tapestry when Angela Dean strolled up and called Kate a loser for hanging out with a freak.

So Kate had slapped her, hard.

Two days later, she apologized to Angela, but the damage was done. Mrs. Dean ordered Kate to leave Timber Ridge. No more riding team, no more—

"You gonna ride today?" Mr. Evans said.

Kate shook her head. She'd only ridden Tapestry once since they moved to Mr. Evans's farm. Even his prize-winning cows were staying inside. They'd churned up the fields and trails into giant ridges of ice; not even a mountain goat could keep its footing out there.

"Maybe I should build an indoor," Mr. Evans said, feeding Pardner the last apple core. "My horse could use the exercise, and so could I." He patted his ample girth. "Now don't forget about that pie. You come and help me eat it, ya hear? And I'll make us some hot chocolate as well."

Kate couldn't refuse.

She wanted to stay in the barn with Tapestry and brush her again, but Mr. Evans was lonely and he'd been beyond generous, letting her stay at his place without paying a cent.

"Five minutes," she said.

He grinned. "Deal."

* * *

After cooling him down, Holly led Magician into his stall. The first thing he did was poke his head over the partition that separated his stall from the empty one beside it. With an anxious whinny he looked around for Tapestry.

"I miss her, too," Holly whispered.

Two weeks ago when Kate left the barn, Aunt Bea had assured both girls she had a foolproof plan to get Kate back at Timber Ridge. All it would take were a few strong words with Mrs. Dean about Angela's despicable behavior, but so far they hadn't worked. When it came to her daughter, Mrs. Dean had a tin ear.

"It's *my* fault," Holly said as she took off Magician's saddle and began to rub him down. "If I hadn't had that dumb fight with Kate, none of this would've happened."

They'd squabbled over Sue's brother. Not because Holly fancied him—she already had a boyfriend—but because Kate had totally blown it when Brad Piretti asked her to the school's Valentine dance. It didn't help that Kate's movie star boyfriend—Nathan Crane—called in the middle of her conversation with Brad.

Talk about bad timing.

Holly cringed as she remembered Kate's meltdown, right there in front of everyone else, including Sue, who was furious that Kate had hurt her brother's feelings. Poor Kate. She was hopeless with boys and Holly only wanted to help. But when she offered advice, Kate accused her of interfering and told her to butt out. Angry and confused,

Holly backed off. Within seconds, Kate had apologized, but Holly stubbornly refused to accept it.

They'd both left the barn in tears.

A week later, they patched things up, but by then it was too late. Kate had run afoul of Angela, gotten herself banned from Timber Ridge, and taken Tapestry over to Mr. Evans's barn.

Mom had tried to intervene.

But Mrs. Dean overruled her, the way she always did. Despite Mom's contract with Timber Ridge to run the barn, teach kids about horses, and produce a first-class riding team, her job mostly depended on keeping Mrs. Dean and Angela happy.

"Hustle," Jennifer said, walking by with an armload of tack. "The others are waiting."

"Okay." Holly planted a kiss on Magician's velvety black nose, threw on his blanket, and scooped up her saddle and bridle. She'd clean them while listening to whatever crazy scheme Jennifer had come up with.

* * *

Sue and Robin gave Holly double high fives the moment she stepped through the tack room door. They'd seen one another at school and had taken riding lessons together, but this was the first time they'd exchanged more than a few words in the past two weeks.

"We're sorry," Sue said, glancing at Robin. "We want

Kate back at Timber Ridge, and we'll do anything to help."

"That's great," Holly said. "But what about Brad?"

School gossip said he was still smarting over Kate's clumsy rejection and he hadn't been near the barn since she left. Still, he hadn't taken Kristina James to the Valentine's dance either, despite Angela's announcement that he would.

"He'll get over it," Sue said, picking a curb chain off the floor and pouring it from one hand to the other. "My brother's a big boy."

Holly bit back a smile. Brad Piretti's shoulders were so wide that it looked as if he was wearing football pads even when he wasn't. At Halloween, he'd dressed as Frankenstein's monster and won the best costume award along with Kate, who'd been voted the ugliest witch. Everyone insisted the winning couple share a kiss, and Kate had to stand on a stool to reach Brad's cheek.

After that, he'd taken her skiing and then felt guilty when she got injured, so he drove her to physical therapy and clucked over her like a mother hen. Brad was a sweet guy, not the tough sports hero everyone else thought he was. He'd also started riding. Holly said it was because he wanted to be near Kate, but she'd insisted Brad was just a friend . . . nothing more.

"Not," Holly insisted. "He's totally into you."

Her words had fallen on deaf ears. Kate's self-confidence with horses was off the charts, but when it came to dating she was worse than a geek with high-waters and a bad haircut.

Straddling a sawhorse, Robin now said, "Any ideas?"

"Yes," Jennifer said. "We give Mrs. Dean an ultimatum." Her voice was so soft, Holly wasn't sure she'd heard her right.

Sue snorted. "Like how?"

"Tell her that we'll quit the riding team if she doesn't let Kate back into the barn."

THERE WAS A STUNNED SILENCE. Sue dropped her curb chain. It clattered onto the floor and made Holly jump.

"You have *got* to be kidding," she said. "Mrs. Dean won't listen to us."

"She will," Jennifer said.

"Why?"

"Because without us, there *is* no riding team," Jennifer said. "Think about it. Liz needs three kids to compete—four is better." She unfolded a metal chair and sat on it backward. "If we bail out, she'd only have Angela and Kristina."

Holly choked back a cry.

This would ruin Mom's reputation. If she lost her job at Timber Ridge, and tried to find another one, the gossip would sink her. She'd be known as the coach whose riding team had quit, and no other barn would hire her.

"Aren't you forgetting something?" Robin said.

Jennifer looked at her. "What?"

"The Festival of Horses," Robin said, running a hand through her dark brown curls. "You guys are competing as individuals. If we all pull out of the team, Mrs. Dean will be thrilled because it'll mean less competition for Angela."

"But that's just for *this* show," Sue pointed out. "What about the others, like the Hampshire Classic? You need to be part of a team. You can't compete as an individual there, and—"

"—it's Mrs. Dean's pet project," Holly finished.

While the others argued, Holly's mind flew back to the previous year's biggest horse show. Thanks to Kate, who'd just arrived at Timber Ridge, they won the Hampshire Classic challenge cup despite Angela's best efforts at sabotage. She didn't give a hoot about the team; she only cared about beating Kate for the individual gold medal. When they were tied for first place, the judge had told them to switch horses for a ride-off.

But Kate backed down.

She refused to let Angela use her spurs on Magician or yank his sensitive mouth. So Angela won her precious medal by default. Holly had known Angela since kindergarten, and she hadn't changed a bit from the spoiled five-year-old who threw a tantrum if another kid got gold stars and she didn't. The stakes were much higher now, the prizes much bigger, and Angela wanted them all.

Holly blamed Mrs. Dean.

She was the worst kind of horse-show mother. She pushed Angela to win at everything—riding, tennis, skiing—no matter the cost. There were times when Holly felt almost sorry for Angela. With a mother like Mrs. Dean, Angela didn't stand a chance of being normal or having real friends. Someone tapped on the tack room door.

"Go away," Jennifer yelled. "We're busy."

Another tap, louder this time.

"I'll get it." Holly scrambled off her tack trunk and cracked open the door. A chestnut pony poked his nose at her.

"Soupy," someone squealed. "Stop it."

A little girl's brown pigtails stuck out from her helmet; her freckled face was flushed as she tugged on her pony's lead rope. He dug in his toes and refused to budge.

"Laura," Holly said, "what do you want?"

"I want you to give these to Soupy." Laura thrust a bag of carrots toward Holly. "Three carrots, twice a day."

It sounded like a doctor's prescription.

"Okay," Holly said, grabbing Laura's carrots and fending off the determined pony. Behind her, the others had stopped talking. "But why?"

"Because I'll be away," Laura said, "and I want my pony to have his treats." Anxiously, she looked at Holly. "Please?"

"Sure," Holly said. "Where are you going?"

"To New York," Laura said. "To see my best friend."

"Marcia?"

But who else would it be? Marcia Dean and Laura Gardner had been inseparable until last Halloween, when Kate and Holly had rescued Marcia from a blizzard and she'd left Timber Ridge to live in New York with her father.

Holly had only met Mr. Dean a couple of times. He was Angela's stepfather and much nicer than his wife. Or were they divorced already? Holly had no idea because Angela never said a word about him, despite the fact that Mr. Dean paid for her horses, her extravagant vacations, the McMansion she lived in, and . . .

A plan began to form in Holly's mind.

"Hold off," she said, the moment Laura clattered down the aisle with her pony.

Sue frowned. "On what?"

"Whatever it is you've been talking about."

"Why?" Robin said.

"Because I've got a better idea."

"Okay, then shoot," Jennifer said.

"Later," Holly replied, not sure if her crazy plan would even work. Bolting from the tack room, she raced toward Laura and her pony. Soupçon's stall was at the far end of the barn.

"I'll need your phone number," Holly said, breathing hard.

"Why?"

"In case Soupy wants to talk to you."

Laura gave an awkward smile. "I don't have a cell phone. Mom says I'm too young."

"Then give me Marcia's," Holly said.

"She doesn't have one, either."

This was working out better than Holly expected. "No problem," she said. "Just give me their land line."

Laura rattled off a string of numbers and Holly crossed her fingers and hoped that she'd actually be able to remember them.

* * *

Kate gave Tapestry's blond mane a quick brush, then put her grooming box in the tack room and headed for Mr. Evan's cute little farmhouse—bright red, just like his barn, with a rope swing on its snow-covered front porch. Kate shucked off her boots at the door before stepping into Mr. Evans's kitchen.

Copper pans hung above a pot-bellied stove, red-checked cushions brightened up the wooden chairs, and matching curtains framed both windows. Another of Aunt Bea's afghans lay across the back of a Boston rocker.

"Is Aunt Bea here?" Kate said.

"She left last night, after dropping off the pie," Mr. Evans said. "One of her book signing tours."

Aunt Bea wrote mysteries and spent half her life traveling around New England promoting them. She'd only known Mr. Evans a short while, but already they'd become quite the couple—like Kate's dad and Holly's mother. Gleefully, Holly had taken all the credit.

"She's a *yenta*," Robin Shapiro had teased.

"What's that?" Kate said.

"A matchmaker," Holly explained, "like in *Fiddler on the Roof*." She adored old movies. One of her favorites was *The Parent Trap*, and it had sparked her idea about getting Liz and Kate's father together. So far, it seemed to be working.

Mr. Evans waved Kate into a chair. "I love having you here."

"Me, too," she said.

Wrapping both hands around a mug of hot chocolate, Kate inhaled the smell of fresh apple pie. Most kids would kill for a gig like this, yet all she wanted was to be back at Timber Ridge.

"But you need to be with your friends," Mr. Evans went on. "You need kids your own age, not an old geezer like me."

Had he just read her mind?

Feeling ungrateful, Kate blushed. "No, no—"

"Quit trying to fool me."

"I'm not," Kate said, blushing even harder.

But the truth was that she had nothing to do at Mr. Evans's barn—nobody to ride with and nowhere to go. At least, not until the ice melted and she could take Tapestry on the trails to meet Holly and the others.

No, not the others.

Except for Jennifer, they were all mad at her. And Kate didn't blame them. Without meaning to, she'd hurt Brad's feelings over the Valentine's Day dance and made everything worse by slapping Angela two days later. Kids at school avoided her, Angela and Kristina spread false rumors, and Kate's grades had begun to suffer. Dad wouldn't be pleased with her next report card unless she buckled down and worked harder.

Mr. Evans pushed a plate toward her. Apple pie with a dollop of vanilla ice cream. "This is a *real* Yankee breakfast," he said.

Gratefully, Kate dug in.

She hadn't eaten since the night before. Not Dad's fault. He'd whipped up a mushroom omelet that morning—courtesy of his cooking lessons with Liz—but had gone to his butterfly museum before Kate crawled out of bed. She didn't fancy cold omelet, so she drank a glass of milk and then slogged up the hill to Mr. Evan's farm. Her cell phone buzzed.

Holly? No, a text from Nathan.

Kate's heart did a slow roll. She hadn't heard from Nathan since his hugely embarrassing call in the middle of Brad's invitation to the school's Valentine dance. It was like Nathan had a sixth sense about Brad. No matter where or when Kate was talking to Brad, Nathan managed to interrupt. It confused Kate and amused Holly, who told her she was lucky to have two guys interested in her.

Where r u? Nathan texted.

The barn, Kate texted back.

As if she'd be anywhere else on a Friday morning in mid-winter break. But Nathan wouldn't know. His world no longer included ordinary things like school schedules and homework and obsessing over that math quiz you flunked last week. Nathan lived in Hollywood, light years away from Kate's tiny village in Vermont.

According to his Facebook page, Nathan was on a publicity tour for the *Moonlight* movie. Kate had met him when part of the film was shot at Timber Ridge the previous summer and she'd ridden as a stunt double for Nathan's glamorous co-star, Tess O'Donnell. Last Kate knew they were in Florida. Some place warm.

Mr. Evans lumbered to his feet. "I have a few cows to take care of, so I'll be at the upper barn if you need anything." The kitchen door closed quietly behind him.

Is it cold? Nathan wrote.

Kate glanced outside. A fringe of icicles hung off Mr. Evans's front porch; snow banks obliterated his truck.

Freezing, she texted.

Warm here, Nathan texted back. *Come down.*

He tossed off invitations like this all the time, even

James L. Hamner Public Library
Amelia Court House, VA 23002

though he knew that Kate couldn't possibly join him. They hadn't seen one another since last September when he went on location and swamped her with texts and phone calls from faraway places like Romania, New Zealand, and Hawaii.

Holly was envious.

So were the kids at school who thought that having a movie-star boyfriend was wicked cool. But they didn't know what it was really like. Something simple, like going out for pizza in the village, turned into a mob-fest when fans recognized Nathan's well-known face.

He shrugged it off, but Kate didn't.

While Nathan happily autographed paper napkins, plastic cups, and even a fan's arm, Kate cringed. She hated the attention, especially when kids who didn't know who she was asked for her autograph as well.

Nathan said it was part of his job.

"But not mine," Kate had said.

And now, when she tried to reply, her thumbs froze. Holly called it being "thumb-tied," except *she* never was. She wasn't ever tongue-tied either. Holly always knew exactly what to say to boys—and everyone else.

* * *

With trembling fingers, Holly punched in Mr. Dean's number. It was eight o'clock on Friday night. Laura would already be there, so surely he'd be at home, too.

But he wasn't.

Cheerfully, Marcia asked if Holly wanted to speak with the babysitter. "We're playing Monopoly and Laura is winning."

"Just tell your dad I called," Holly said. "And ask him to call me back."

"Okay," Marcia said and hung up.

Holly slumped in her chair. Marcia would never remember to tell her dad that she'd called, and even if she did, he probably wouldn't call back. Holly doubted he'd even remember her. When they rescued Marcia, it was Kate's name that got his attention because she'd stayed with Marcia while Holly rode off to get help.

Okay, now what?

Plan A wasn't going too well, but Holly didn't have a Plan B. Somehow, there had to be a way of getting Kate back to the barn that didn't involve Angela's mother.

But Holly couldn't think of one.

When it came to Timber Ridge and the riding team, Mrs. Dean's beaky nose was everywhere. It was so sharp, it could cut paper. Holly wasn't sure that even Mr. Dean could escape it. He may have been a financial genius on Wall Street, but he was no match for his wife. Nobody else was, either.

To Holly's surprise, he called at ten the next morning. "Sorry I missed your call last night," Mr. Dean said, sounding friendly and cheerful. "What's up?"

Holly's tongue froze—just like Kate's fingers always did when she had to text with Nathan. "Mrs. Dean has banned Kate from the barn," Holly blurted. "She's off the riding team."

"Why?"

So Holly told him.

She left nothing out, not even Kate slapping Angela. It was a huge risk—asking for another favor—but Mr. Dean had been so grateful when they'd rescued Marcia from the blizzard that he'd promised to help in any way he could. Last fall he'd gotten his wife to drop Angela's trumped-up charges against Kate for trampling their front lawn and had arranged financing so Kate's father could buy the butterfly museum. Maybe that was enough. Maybe he thought he'd already fulfilled his obligation.

"I'll take care of it," he said.

Holly's breath came out in a rush. "Seriously?"

"Yes, seriously," he said. "Don't worry about it. We'll have Kate back on the team in a jiffy."

Holly wasn't sure what a jiffy was, but it sounded pretty cool.

"Wow," she said, wanting to hug him. But that would have to wait until she and Kate went to New York for the *Moonlight* premiere in April. Nathan had sent them tickets and Holly hoped he wouldn't let Kate down when he saw her.

The gossip mags said otherwise.

They'd plastered pictures of Nathan and his co-star Tess O'Donnell on the web so many times that even Kate was starting to worry, though she hadn't said a word.

Holly clenched both fists.

Never mind that Nathan Crane was her favorite movie star, she would totally deck him if he ever hurt Kate.

3

"Wow," Jennifer said, when Holly shared her news about Angela's stepfather going to bat for them over Kate. "Looks like we're good to go."

"When?" Sue said.

"Don't know," Holly said. She hadn't said a word about this to her mother and hoped that Mrs. Dean wouldn't drag her feet over telling Mom to re-instate Kate at Timber Ridge.

No questions asked.

But Holly would be only too happy to answer questions. She would tell Mom about all of it the moment Mrs. Dean called. It might take a while, but hopefully it would be before Kate's fifteenth birthday in two weeks.

It would be the best gift ever. She'd already begged Aunt Bea to crochet an ear bonnet for Tapestry because it was her birthday, too.

"We'll have a party," Jennifer said, "for both of them."

"A double feature?" Holly said.

"Perfect," Sue exclaimed. "But where?"

"In the barn," Holly said. "With all our horses and silly games and—"

"Surprise guests?" Jennifer went on.

Quietly, Robin said, "Let's invite Nathan."

"He's away," Holly said.

"Then he can fly home," Sue said, fluffing up her sandy red hair. It stuck out behind both ears and made her look like a squirrel. "He can afford it, plus he used to live in Vermont. It's not like he'd be coming to another planet."

Holly added his name to her list, but she knew Nathan wouldn't come. Neither would Angela and Kristina, whom Jennifer insisted she also invite.

"As a safeguard," she said.

They hadn't been asked to Holly's birthday in November. So they'd gate-crashed it and set off all the fire alarms, and Holly didn't want that happening again. Reluctantly, she wrote their names on her list. She added Brad's name, too, but had no idea if he'd accept.

He was probably still sore about Kate.

In the end, they wound up with invitations for eight girls and four guys, including Holly's boyfriend, Adam, who rode for Larchwood, one of Timber Ridge's biggest competitors.

"Plus Aunt Bea, Liz, Mr. Evans, and Kate's father," Jennifer said.

Holly added them to her list.

They agreed to keep it a surprise. On Kate's birthday, Liz would truck Tapestry back to the Timber Ridge barn while Jennifer kept Kate busy.

"Where will you take her?" Sue asked.

Jennifer thought for a minute. "The mall?"

"Dream on," Holly said. "When's the last time Kate even looked at cute clothes?"

"What about Winfield Tack?" Robin said.

"That'll only take an hour," Sue said. "We need to get her away, like *far* away."

Nobody had any good ideas until Holly checked her iPhone and said, "How about a Lockie Malone clinic? She'll be all over it."

Lockie Malone had given a clinic at their barn in January, but Kate hadn't been able to ride in it because of her bad knee.

"Without Tapestry?" Sue said.

"Yes," Holly said. "This one's a demo at Fox Meadow Farm. Just Lockie Malone, a couple of other trainers, and their grand prix horses."

"Cool beans," Jennifer said. "Who will take her?"

"Liz?" Robin said.

Sue shook her head. "She'll be trucking Tapestry."

"But Aunt Bea won't," Holly said.

The others gave her high fives for solving the problem. Now all they had to do was cross their fingers and hope that Angela's stepfather wouldn't fail them.

* * *

Finally, two days before Kate's birthday, Mrs. Dean called. Holly only heard her mother's side of the conversation but had no trouble imagining Mrs. Dean's pencil-thin eyebrows twisting themselves into knots as she struggled to say the words she didn't want to say. The moment Mom hung up, she pinned Holly with a look.

It all spilled out—Aunt Bea's failed blackmail with Mrs. Dean, Jennifer's whacko idea about them quitting the team, and finally Holly's brainwave to get Mr. Dean involved.

"Sneaky," her mother said.

Holly grinned. "But it worked, right?"

"I feel bad that I couldn't get Kate back on the team without all this fuss," Liz said. "But—"

"It's okay. I understand," Holly said, hugging her.

More than once, Mom had risked her job—and the house that came with it—by going head-to-head with Mrs. Dean. From the beginning, Mom had fought for Kate and had spent countless hours coaching Angela, trying to help her fulfill her mother's expectations, even though Angela blew off most of Mom's advice.

Then came Ragtime.

With bling on his hooves and a flashy gold halter, he'd sashayed into the Timber Ridge barn like a rock star. Angela wasn't even there. She had no idea her mother had replaced her old horse, Skywalker, with a brand spanking new one that cost a small fortune.

Despite his outrageous price tag, Ragtime stuck his friendly nose into the aisle and frisked anyone passing by in the hopes of scoring a treat. Everyone, except Angela, loved him.

* * *

After the last visitors left her father's butterfly museum, Kate locked its front door. Then she turned off the spotlight that shone above the sign, "Dancing Wings." It showed a butterfly in ballet slippers and a gaudy pink tutu that Kate figured Dad would have changed by now. But he hadn't. He hadn't said a word about her birthday, either. Maybe he'd forgotten about it.

No surprise there.

Her father rarely remembered anything unless it had wings, fuzzy legs, and compound eyes. Ben MacGregor was one of the world's leading lepidopterists, but when it came to kids, he didn't have a clue. Maybe tonight he'd say something, like suggest they go out for pizza or a movie.

Kate's cell phone buzzed.

Aunt Bea said, "Are you free tomorrow?"

"Why?" Kate said.

There was a pause. "Because it's your birthday and I'd like to take you somewhere special."

Dad was behind the gift shop counter, rounding up stray puzzle pieces and untangling the legs of a wire-frame caterpillar. His assistant, Mrs. Gordon, was re-shelving books, including Dad's surprise bestseller, *The Shy Butterfly*. Much to Kate's delight, Dad's new picture book was such a hit, parents and kids had lined up for his autograph.

"I can't," Kate said.

She'd promised Dad a whole day at the museum. Saturday was their busiest day—biology students from UVM and skiers who'd gotten tired of fighting lift lines on the mountain.

"Go," Dad said.

Kate looked at him. Had he heard Aunt Bea's voice or had she called him earlier to ask permission? You never knew with grownups.

"Are you sure?" Kate said.

Mrs. Gordon chimed in. "We'll do fine without you, Kate. Just go along with Aunt Bea, and—"

It sounded like a conspiracy.

But that was crazy. Kate only had two friends. Holly and Jennifer couldn't possibly pull off a surprise party the way Kate had for Holly's birthday last November when everyone had pitched in.

"Okay," she told Aunt Bea. "I'd love it."

"Then I'll pick you up at eight."

Knowing Aunt Bea, they could be doing anything from visiting a grizzled sheep farmer to checking out a woman who spun yarn or hand-dyed fabric to make quilts. The last thing Kate expected was a dressage clinic with Lockie Malone.

* * *

Holly swung into high gear, barking out orders like a drill sergeant. Mr. Evans had volunteered to truck Tapestry over, so that freed up Mom to teach her regular lessons. Jennifer arrived with a boatload of decorations—everything from balloons to banners to birthday hats.

Sue stripped Tapestry's stall.

Her brother lugged two bales of fresh shavings from the feed room. Clued in by Sue, Holly didn't say a word except, "Hey, Brad. Good to see you."

But there was no word from Nathan, not even a text message that said he knew it was Kate's birthday. Disappointed, Holly helped Robin muck stalls and sweep the aisle, but when Adam arrived with Domino—his half-Arabian pinto—Holly abandoned her broom and badgered Adam for news about Nathan.

They were best friends.

Before Nathan hit the big time in Hollywood, he'd gone to high school with Adam. Surely Adam would know what was going on. But he didn't. Closing Domino's stall door, he leaned over and kissed Holly's cheek.

"Sorry, but I'm out of Nathan's loop."

Holly felt herself deflate. Even though inviting Nathan to Kate's birthday was a long shot, she'd held out hope that he'd turn up at the last minute the way he had at last year's Labor Day costume party. Holly had masterminded the subterfuge and sworn Adam to secrecy.

Kate had no idea Nathan was coming then. But the look on her face was totally worth all the work when Nathan emerged from the back end of Adam's crazy horse outfit. Yesterday, Jennifer had suggested they do the same for Kate.

"I love costume parties," Robin said.

Sue clapped. "Me, too."

"Not enough time," Holly said.

Her own amazingly wonderful surprise birthday had involved glamorous gowns, movie posters, and guys in tuxedos. It had taken Kate and Adam three weeks to pull off and Holly had loved every minute of it.

But Holly didn't have that option with Kate.

Thanks to Mrs. Dean dragging her feet, they now had less than forty-eight hours to order food, organize a bunch of games, and get all the props ready—sacks for musical chairs, eggs and spoons, and Kate's favorite, apple bobbing.

Jennifer added another game.

"The hobo race," she said, hefting a carton of old clothes into the arena.

"What's all this about?" Holly said.

"Trust me," Jennifer said. "You'll love it."

Just then, the barn door opened.

Holly whipped around and let out a happy cry. There was Tapestry, ears pricked and whickering softly. Holly stepped forward and took the mare's lead rope from Mr. Evans.

"Thank you," she said.

He grinned. "My pleasure."

It seemed as if the entire barn lit up when Holly led Tapestry down the aisle. Horses whinnied, kids cheered, and parents took videos. If only Kate could see this in real time—especially the moment when Tapestry touched Magician's nose.

They squealed, they kissed.

Adam put his arm around Holly's shoulders. "Well done," he whispered.

* * *

The Fox Meadow indoor was bigger than Kate remembered, and it was filled with eager spectators, many of them sporting shamrock pins, green scarves, and shiny green hats. Aunt Bea snagged two box seats, right by the in-gate. When Lockie Malone entered the arena, he stopped in front of Kate.

She almost died.

"I remember you," he said. "How's your knee?"

"It's great," Kate said, wishing her tongue wasn't tangled up with her teeth.

"Did you make that qualifying show?"

"Yes," she choked out.

"Then I'll be watching for you in April."

Kate was too embarrassed to tell him she wouldn't be going. With a nod, Lockie turned and strode across the tanbark toward his two horses, both ridden by girls Kate thought she recognized but couldn't quite place. Her program said Greer Swope and Talia Margolin from Bittersweet Farm.

"Half sisters," Aunt Bea whispered. "They're really good."

The morning passed in a blur of flying changes, leg yields, and half passes, with Lockie Malone emphasizing the importance of balance and invisible aids. He explained that dressage was about the rider being in a different place in the saddle than when riding hunt seat.

Lunch was even more amazing.

Aunt Bea had wangled invitations to the officials' tent, where St. Patrick's Day celebrations were in full swing with buckets of green popcorn on every table and sparkly shamrocks stuck on all the chairs. Lockie Malone and his two riders were tucking into corned beef and cabbage.

Kate couldn't take her eyes off them.

At eighteen, Greer Swope was making a name for herself on the Florida jumper circuit. Talia Margolin was a solid dressage rider who also coached kids and their ponies. She looked up and caught Kate's eye.

"Happy birthday," she whispered.

How did she know?

Greer said, "Look behind you."

Kate turned, and there was Aunt Bea, holding out a small cake with green frosting and a bright green candle on top. Someone broke into the *Happy Birthday* song, and then everyone joined in. Lockie Malone had a surprisingly good voice.

"Blow out your candle and make a wish," Aunt Bea said.

So Kate did.

* * *

By five o'clock, everything was ready. Robin's mother had organized the food, including two enormous carrot cakes—one piled high with cream cheese frosting for Kate's birthday and the other with carrot chunks on top for Tapestry. Chips and salsa, fruit punch, platters of raw veggies, and Mrs. West's famous mini-quiches sat on a table outside the tack room. Beside it was a bucket of carrots. Pizza would be delivered later.

Plug, the barn's smallest pony, couldn't wait. He didn't care about pizza; he just wanted a carrot. Despite Marcia Dean's best efforts, Plug dragged her down the aisle and helped himself, with Soupy right behind him.

Holly rescued the bucket, then banished both ponies and their riders from the barn. Laughing, she pointed at the indoor. "Go and practice for the games in there."

Laura giggled. "C'mon Marcia."

Marcia, Laura's best friend, was here for Kate's birthday and Holly loved seeing the two little girls together again. They were the next generation of Timber Ridge riders. Last year they'd won ribbons in the walk-trot division. This season, they'd be cantering and taking small jumps.

Slowly, the other guests trickled in. Holly made sure everyone parked behind the barn so Kate wouldn't see their cars. Then Jennifer's new boyfriend, Gus Underwood, showed up with a guitar slung over one shoulder. His band had rocked the walls at last month's Valentine's dance.

"No amps," Jennifer warned. "You'll scare the horses."

"No problem," he said, patting his shiny brown Yamaha. "This one's acoustic."

Gus offered to handle the music, so Holly took him into the arena's observation room, where she'd set up chairs for the grownups.

"The sound system's in that closet," she said, pointing to a narrow door with a small dusty window. "We've got lots of CDs, so choose whatever works for the games we're playing. Just not too loud, okay?"

"The horses?" Gus said.

Holly grinned. "*And* the parents."

Robin and Sue set up traffic cones, Adam helped to move jumps, and Jennifer gave Laura and Marcia tubes of green glitter.

"Decorate your ponies," she said.

"And Rebel?" Laura said.

Jennifer nodded. "Sure, he'd love it."

"Keep it away from their eyes and ears," Liz warned, as the girls ran off. "And keep it out of my office. I don't want to find glitter in my coffeepot tomorrow morning."

"They're here," Sue yelled.

Holly felt a twinge of doubt. Had she done the right thing? Did Kate really want to come back to Timber Ridge after all the recent trauma? So far, there was no sign of Angela or Kristina. Or Brad, either. He'd quietly disappeared.

"Okay," Holly said. "Action stations."

Kids darted into stalls, grown-ups crammed into Liz's office, and Mrs. West draped a plastic cloth over the food table so it wouldn't be quite so obvious. Holly stationed herself beside Tapestry.

"Not long now, girl," she whispered.

4

AS THEY DROVE BACK TO WINFIELD, Kate rehashed every detail of Lockie Malone's clinic that she could remember. If only she could take one with Tapestry. They would learn so much more.

"Maybe next time," Aunt Bea said.

Kate remembered her manners. "Thank you. This was the best birthday gift ever."

"Despite the corned beef and cabbage?"

"It was delicious," Kate said.

Aunt Bea patted the shamrock sticker on her windshield. "It's tough, isn't it?"

"What is?"

"Having a birthday close to a holiday."

"I guess," Kate said.

St. Patrick's Day was still two days off, but Sue Piretti

had it worse. Her birthday was December 25th and she
never got separate presents—just a big one that her family
said covered both occasions. Kate had given her two—a
Barn Bratz t-shirt wrapped in Santa Claus paper and a
pair of Thelwell Pony socks bundled up in yellow tissue.
Given what happened later with Brad, Sue had probably
stuffed Kate's gifts into a drawer or even tossed them out.

"When's your birthday?" Kate asked Aunt Bea.

"Easter Sunday."

"But that changes every year," Kate said, running
through her mental calendar. "It's never the same."

Aunt Bea grinned. "Neither is my age."

Holly said it was a closely guarded secret, like some of
Aunt Bea's knitting patterns, which looked like hiero-
glyphics to Kate. She glanced at Aunt Bea's quilted bag.
Wooden needles sprouted from a huge ball of fuzzy blue
yarn.

"How's the bunny?" Kate said.

Aunt Bea had been knitting a blue rabbit for the past
three months. Kate figured it had to be the size of a giraffe
by now.

"Coming along."

"I wish I could knit," Kate said.

Her hands were nimble with a horse's reins but hopeless when it came to yarn and needles. Instructions like
K2, Sl1, and *PSSO* turned Kate's fingers into lumps of
clay.

Holly had interpreted. "It's *knit two, slip one, and pass the slipped stitch over*," she'd said, working furiously on a multicolored scarf that twisted in all directions like a Mobius strip.

"Knitting is about memorizing sequences," Aunt Bea said.

"Like math?"

"And music," Aunt Bea replied, turning off the highway. "All it takes is dedication and practice." She paused. "And a smidgeon of raw talent."

"I've got ten thumbs."

"Nonsense," said Aunt Bea. "You ride dressage."

Lights glowed in shop windows as they drove down Main Street. Slowly, they passed Winfield Tack, the pharmacy, and Blaines, the snooty boutique where Angela bought her designer clothes. But two blocks further on, Kate's cottage was shrouded in darkness. No sign of life, not even a light on their front porch. Was her father still at Dancing Wings?

Kate felt a pang of guilt.

Tomorrow, she would work at Dad's museum, and she'd get all her homework done as well. Plus she'd study extra hard for next week's algebra quiz. The village's lone traffic light turned red.

Aunt Bea slid to a halt.

"Thanks for a wonderful birthday," Kate said, scooping up her knapsack. She checked inside to make sure the program that Lockie Malone had autographed was still there. "You can drop me off here."

Aunt Bea stepped on the gas. "No time."

"Why?" Kate said.

Her cottage whizzed by. So did her high school and the fire department, and in no time they were careening up the hill toward Timber Ridge at twice the posted speed limit. Hands clenched on the wheel, Aunt Bea swerved to avoid a snowplow, then narrowly missed an SUV filled with skiers coming the other way. Kate tightened her seatbelt.

It was worse than driving with Dad.

Several turns later they pulled into the barn's empty parking lot. Aunt Bea slammed on her brakes and almost skidded into a fence post. Kate braced herself on the dashboard.

"Why are we here?" she said, shaking.

"I left my yarn in Liz's office."

Kate stared at her. "Like you don't have enough?"

"Don't be cheeky," Aunt Bea said, yanking off her hat. "Your legs are younger than mine, so run in and get it for me, okay?" A halo of frizzy red hair framed Aunt Bea's face and reminded Kate of Ms. Frizzle in *The Magic School Bus*, except Kate reckoned that Ms. Frizzle was a much better driver.

"I can't."

"Why not?"

"Because—" Kate sucked in her breath. This was the first time she'd been at Timber Ridge since the night four weeks ago when she'd crept in like a thief to collect her tack, her helmet, and her grooming box.

"Don't worry," Aunt Bea said. "Nobody's here."

Except for a lone floodlight, the barn looked empty and deserted. Kate checked her watch. Almost six. Liz and Holly must've fed the horses early tonight. "All right," she said.

"Thank you." Aunt Bea shifted awkwardly in her seat. "My bones are way too old and creaky."

"Liar," Kate said, grinning.

Holly's aunt had more energy than all the barn kids put together. Years ago, she'd run a successful breeding farm, trained show horses, and been a fairy godmother to countless riders, including Liz. And as if that weren't enough, Aunt Bea was now a bestselling author.

She patted Kate's knee. "Humor me."

"Okay."

Negotiating snowdrifts, Kate headed for the barn. She opened the side door and stepped inside, then waited for her eyes to adjust. In the gloom, everything looked the same, yet slightly different. The barn's familiar old wheelbarrow sported a dozen shamrock stickers and someone—probably Jennifer—had twisted green ribbons around the rakes, brooms, and pitchforks that hung on the wall.

Horses rattled buckets.

Whickering hopefully, Plug stuck his cute little nose over the stall door he could barely reach.

"Sorry guy," Kate said. "No treats for you."

They'd almost lost Plug to colic the previous month when he got Ragtime's feed by mistake. In the next stall, Laura's chestnut pony was munching hay. Was that green glitter on Soupy's hindquarters? Kate looked closer.

Yup, glitter.

Sadness overwhelmed her, a feeling of loss. This was what Kate missed—the fun and crazy parties, cheering for her friends at horse shows, and the heart-stopping moments of intense competition. But most of all, she missed Holly. They'd had a couple of sleepovers and Holly had helped at Dad's museum last Sunday, but it wasn't the same any more—not with Kate and Tapestry at Mr. Evans's barn and Holly still here with Magician.

Slowly, Kate approached his stall, eyes averted from the one beside it where Tapestry used to live. In the dim light, Kate could just about see Holly's black horse. He whickered, the way Plug had done, and as Kate reached out to stroke Magician's nose, the barn lights came on.

All at once.

* * *

"*Surprise!*" yelled a chorus of voices.

"Happy birthday," Jennifer yelled.

"Welcome home," shouted Robin and Sue.

In a daze, Kate whirled around and there were Aunt Bea, Dad, and Mrs. Gordon right behind her.

Where had they come from?

Aunt Bea grinned. "You can forget about my yarn."

Grabbing Kate's hands, Adam swung her in circles, then passed her onto Liz who pulled her into a bone-crunching hug. Laura squealed; Marcia squealed even louder. With a huge grin, Jennifer thumped Kate's back so hard that she almost fell over. In the midst of it all, she heard a familiar whicker.

"Tapestry?" she choked out.

Holly's blue eyes sparkled. "Yes."

More cheers erupted as Holly led Tapestry into the aisle. Ears pricked, Kate's golden mare floated toward her. Blue and green ribbons fluttered from Tapestry's silvery mane; a giant blue bow glittering with stars spilled across her withers. Even Tapestry's hooves glistened. For a moment, Kate just stood there unable to move. She opened her mouth, then shut it again.

Then she burst into tears.

* * *

Holly handed Kate a wet paper towel. "You're a hot mess."

"Thanks," Kate said.

"For the towel or the insult?"

"Both," Kate said, peering at herself in the tack room's tiny mirror. Its cracked surface turned her green eyes and flushed cheeks into a kaleidoscope. She wiped her face, then finger-combed her thick brown hair, glad she'd washed it that morning.

"Much better," Holly said, opening the door. "You ready to face the masses again?"

"Who's coming?" Kate said.

Would Nathan show up? Had Holly even invited him? And what about Brad? The last time she'd seen him at school he'd walked right past her.

"The usual crowd," Holly said.

Not much help there. With a sigh, Kate crumpled up her paper towel and tossed it into the overflowing bin. Tomorrow she would empty it, and she'd sweep the tack room—that is, if Dad didn't need her at the museum.

He stood at the food table with his arm draped casually around Liz's shoulders. They looked so comfortable, so right together that Kate found it hard to believe they'd only known one another since last October. They had met at the Halloween hunter pace and ever since then, Holly had been on a mission to get them together—as in *married*—with a white wedding and Kate and Holly as bridesmaids.

"So we can be *real* sisters," she'd said.

Kate wanted it, too . . . desperately.

But it didn't take much to split families and best

friends apart. She'd learned that with Holly . . . and with Angela and her stepsister, Marcia, too. Blended families didn't always work out the way you wanted them to.

Holly reached for Kate's hand. "C'mon."

"No, wait," Kate said, pulling herself away. "How did you—? I mean, *who*—?"

She waved toward her grooming box, sitting beside her tack trunk. On the rack above were Tapestry's saddle and bridle. Her blue cooler lay folded across a sawhorse. Everything was back where it belonged, including Kate's helmet and spare riding boots.

"Elves," Holly said.

"Be serious," Kate said. "It was Aunt Bea, right?"

"Nope."

"Then who?"

"The Wizard of Wall Street," Holly said. "He had a few choice words with his soon-to-be-former wife, the Wicked Witch of Timber Ridge."

"Mr. Dean?" Kate gasped.

Holly slapped her a high five. "Now, let's go," she said. "We have games to play."

* * *

The music stopped and Kate galloped toward the last sack. She threw herself off Tapestry, but Sue got there first. They rolled about in the tanbark, laughing. Then came the egg-and-spoon race, which Adam won.

"You cheated," Holly said.

With a sheepish grin, Adam turned his wooden spoon upside down. The plastic egg didn't move. Holly grabbed it.

"Chewing gum," she said. "Disgusting."

"Dude," Gus said, slapping Adam on the back.

Robin rode up beside Kate. "You'll win the next race."

"What is it?"

"Apple bobbing."

"I won't, but Tapestry will," Kate said.

She couldn't stop smiling. It wasn't just the crazy games and Jennifer's green cloak and top hat that made her look like an Irish ringmaster, it was everything—the barn, the horses, and the inescapable feeling that she really had come home. Her mood didn't even falter when Angela and Kristina showed up.

Holly groaned. "I had to invite them."

"It's okay," Kate said. "I can deal."

Being back at Timber Ridge meant working *with* Angela, not against her. Kate resolved to do much better this time.

"Sorry we're late," Angela drawled. "It took, like, for*ever* to get back from the clinic."

"You were there?" Kate said. "I didn't see you."

"That's because we were in the officials' tent."

"So was I," Kate said. "With Aunt Bea. We sat near Lockie Malone and—"

"Oh, *him*," Angela scoffed. "He's nothing."

Kate opened her mouth and shut it again. No point in reminding Angela that Lockie Malone had found Ragtime for Mrs. Dean. It was odd, the way Angela and Ragtime hadn't clicked. Not that she'd clicked that well with Skywalker, either. Maybe Angela didn't like horses very much and only rode them to please her demanding mother.

"So where were you?" Robin asked.

"At a George Morris clinic." Angela tossed a wave of black hair over one shoulder. "He's way more famous than a two-bit trainer from—"

"Listen up, everyone," Jennifer said, pointing at a basket of Granny Smith apples like the ones Aunt Bea used in her famous pies. "We're gonna run the apple bobbing in two heats. We've got ten riders and five buckets, and—"

"—not enough apples," Sue said as Plug helped himself to the basket that Jennifer wasn't paying any attention to.

"Marcia, control your pony," Angela said.

Marcia stuck out her tongue. "*You* try."

"Here's the deal," Jennifer said, handing out plastic ponchos. "Put these on, then ride as fast as you can to the bucket."

"Why the ponchos?" Angela said.

Holly grinned. "Because you'll get wet."

Angela dropped hers on the ground. "Then count me out."

"Me, too," said Kristina. "This is kindergarten stuff."

"Who's supposed to bob for the apple?" Robin said, patting Chantilly's dappled gray neck. "Me or my horse?"

"You," Jennifer said. "With your teeth. Both hands behind your back."

"What if Tilly gets it first?"

"Then you're disqualified," Jennifer said.

She told Gus and Adam to fill the buckets with water and space them out. "Once you've got the apple, get on your horse and race back."

Liz produced replacement apples, and the first heat began. Marcia and Laura didn't stand a chance. Before they even jumped off their ponies Plug and Soupy had already stuck their noses deep into the buckets and snarfed up the apples. Water sloshed everywhere; Plug slobbered juice down the front of Marcia's hoodie.

"Lesson learned," Robin said to Kate. "Get off your horse *before* you reach the bucket."

Holly ended up winning the heat, with Sue close behind on Tara, her Appaloosa mare.

"Our turn," Jennifer said.

She lined up with Adam, Robin, and Kate while Gus dropped another apple into each bucket.

Liz yelled, "*Go!*"

Kate was in the lead, halfway to her bucket, when Brad showed up and blew her concentration to bits. Sensing victory, Tapestry took control and snagged the apple. But Kate didn't care. Something inside her lightened.

"Hi," Brad said, waving from the doorway.

Feeling awkward, she waved back. "Hi."

Now what? Ride toward him, play it cool, or—?

Her cell phone rang. Kate pulled it from her pocket, checked caller ID, and promptly turned if off. This time, Nathan Crane could wait until later.

5

JENNIFER CALLED FOR A BREAK. She'd just beaten Holly in the apple-bobbing final and was sharing her prize with Rebel when Gus yelled that the pizza had arrived.

Kate sniffed. "Pepperoni?"

"Your favorite," Holly said, feeling smug. "With mushrooms and extra cheese."

There was a mad dash for the barn. Chips and salsa disappeared, Mrs. West's mini-quiches vanished like magic, and Holly cheered when Kate beat Sue's brother for the last slice of pizza. With a grin, Brad opened another box. This was turning into a great party. Even Angela's unexpected arrival hadn't spoiled it—yet.

As if reading her mind, Kate said, "Why do you suppose Angela came?"

"To cause trouble?" Melted cheese dribbled down Holly's chin.

Kate thrust a napkin at her. "Or maybe she was told to."

"Who by?"

"Mr. Dean," Kate said. "Think about it. He pays for everything. Without him, Angela has nothing. Neither does Mrs. Dean."

Holly hadn't thought of that. To her, Angela had always been the rich kid, the girl who got everything she asked for. Until Marcia spilled a few family secrets last fall, nobody even knew she was Angela's stepsister. It explained a lot, like why Mrs. Dean and Angela had been so mean to her.

"Do you suppose they'll have to move?" Holly said.

"I doubt it," Kate said. "Mr. Dean's a nice guy. I don't think he'd force them out, you know, after the divorce. But I bet he's told Angela to clean up her act."

Holly snorted. "And pigs will fly."

* * *

Following Holly back into the arena, Kate and the others gathered around Jennifer as she explained the hobo race.

"We'll have two teams, and you're the captains," she said pointing at Angela and Kristina. "Pick one person each, then that person will pick another, and—"

"Us?" Angela said, looking surprised.

But Kate wasn't. Jennifer had already warned her

she'd be choosing Angela and Kristina as team leaders. *Damage control*, she'd called it.

Kristina pulled a face. "Who died and left you in charge?"

"Nobody," Holly snapped "If you don't like it, don't play."

"I don't even know what it is," Kristina said.

Sue grinned. "Me, neither."

Ignoring them, Jennifer upended her box of old clothes. "There are two sets of everything," she said, as baggy pants with suspenders, oversized shirts, rubber boots, gardening gloves, and straw hats tumbled out. "You race to your team's pile, get dressed, and lead your horse around the traffic cones. Then you take off your stuff, ride back to your team, and tag the next person to go."

"Like a relay race?" Robin said.

Jennifer nodded. "And one more thing: The last riders keep their hobo clothes on. They can either run back or ride their horses"—she gave a wicked grin—"*if* they can get on."

Brad picked up a boot. "I'll never fit in this."

"Then I'm not choosing you," Angela said.

"I will," said Kristina.

"You can't," Holly said. "He doesn't have a horse."

"He does now," her mother said, leading Marmalade into the arena. At seventeen hands, the half-Percheron chestnut was the barn's biggest horse. Nobody knew what the other half was.

"Hold up a minute," Jennifer said, looking stricken. "I forgot about Gus. He doesn't ride."

"Yes, I do," he said.

Jennifer's eyebrows shot up. "You never said."

"You never asked."

"Western?" Kate said. She couldn't picture Gus Underwood riding English. He was too casual, too laid back—more like a cowboy than a show jumper.

He shrugged. "A little dude ranch stuff."

"Cool beans," Jennifer said. "Let's get Daisy."

"I'm on it," Liz said.

Five minutes later she returned with riding helmets for Brad and Gus, and leading Daisy tacked up in the Western saddle that Mr. Evans had loaned to Aunt Bea. She said it was much easier on her creaky old bones.

Magician whinnied. He'd been Daisy's best buddy until last summer when Tapestry arrived. She gave a little snort and flicked her ears.

"Jealous?" Kate said, patting her.

"No, but I am," Brad said.

Kate turned away to hide her blush. Had Brad guessed her call was from Nathan? Even Holly hadn't noticed, and she had eyes like a hawk.

"Okay," Jennifer said. "Time to pick teams. Angela, you go first."

Kate shared a look with Holly.

Angela? Playing silly games?

Then again, her beady-eyed mother wasn't watching.

Maybe that was the answer. If Mrs. Dean wasn't around to slam Angela for not winning, Angela could relax and enjoy herself.

"Gus," Angela said.

He gave a thumbs-up. "First-draft pick."

"Go, dude," Adam said. "You're—"

Kristina cut him off. "I want Brad."

Predictably, Gus chose Jennifer, and Kate waited for Brad to choose her, but he picked Marcia instead. With a delighted squeal, she skipped toward him dragging a reluctant Plug. After that, the choices went fast. Robin, Holly and Adam wound up on Kristina's team, which left Laura, Sue, and Kate with Angela.

Could they really work together this time?

Just for fun?

Kate glanced at the observation room, filled with smiling grown-ups. No sign of Mrs. Dean, so Angela stood a chance. For a moment, they locked eyes—two girls on the same team and determined to win.

* * *

Angela took charge. She lined up her riders—Gus in front and Kate at the end. "You're the anchor," she said. "Don't mess it up."

"Aye, aye, captain." Kate said.

She glanced at Kristina's team and saw that Holly was their anchor. If nobody flubbed up, they'd be going head-to-head at the end. Holly grinned and gave her a thumbs-up.

"No cavorting with the enemy," Gus warned.

He looked really cute on Daisy. Had a nice seat, too—relaxed and easy, with one hand resting on the pommel. Kate figured he'd probably done a little more than just dude ranch riding.

And then they were off. Gus and Brad raced for the piles, and, sure enough Brad couldn't get the boots on properly. Gus had Daisy around the traffic cones before Brad shoved his straw hat on.

"Scarecrow!" someone yelled.

"Where's the Tin Man?"

Cheers, boos, and whistles rang out as Gus beat Brad by three lengths. But Marcia made up for it. Racing against Laura, she closed the gap, and by the time Sue and Robin faced off, the teams were even again. Jennifer and Adam were next to go.

"Good luck," Kate said.

Jennifer grinned. "No worries."

The moment Sue tagged her, she was off. Rebel skidded to a halt at the pile, then promptly grabbed the straw hat with his teeth.

"No," Jennifer cried, snatching it back. "It's not a snack."

The audience roared.

Kate glanced at her dad. He was doubled over with

laughter. Aunt Bea was on her feet, brandishing her knitting needles. Liz had a silly grin on her face.

"Go, Rebel," Brad yelled.

Pants on backward, Adam tripped over his boots, then lost a glove when he tried to get up. Domino, clearly miffed at being outdone by Rebel, nudged Adam with his nose and he went flying again.

"C'mon, Jen," Angela cried.

Jennifer stumbled around the cones, ripped off her shirt, and jumped out of her boots. Amid cheers and jeers, Adam caught up with her halfway back to home base, surged ahead, and tagged Kristina a few precious seconds before Jennifer tagged Angela.

Ragtime launched himself like a catapult. In three strides he was neck-and-neck with Cody. Both girls landed on the clothes together—pants on first, then the shirt. Angela had trouble with the boots; Kristina couldn't find the second glove.

"Hustle!" Jennifer yelled.

Kate bit her lip. This was worse than a timed jump-off. Straw hats wobbling on top of their riding helmets, both girls dragged their horses around the cones. They shucked off their clothes. It took Angela longer than Kristina.

What was she doing? Folding laundry?

Moments later, Kate found out. She thrust both legs through the pants, straight into her boots like firemen did.

Score one for Angela.

But it didn't stop there. Angela had made sure the shirt sleeves weren't tangled up. In a flash, Kate had it on, then the gloves and straw hat, while Holly was still struggling with hers. Kate looped the suspenders over her shoulders and led Tapestry around the cones.

Decision time.

Run back or ride Tapestry?

Riding was a whole lot faster, but getting on was a challenge. The boots wouldn't fit in the stirrups and the baggy pants made it impossible to vault. From the corner of her eye, Kate could see that Holly was having the same problem. Magician stood at sixteen hands; Tapestry was an inch shorter. It wasn't as if the horses would lie down and—

Duh-uh.

Kate felt like an idiot.

In a flash, she whipped off Tapestry's saddle, then pointed at her shoulder. "Down."

The barn kids loved this trick, and it had helped save Marcia when Kate found her in the blizzard. She'd made Tapestry lie down so that she and Marcia could snuggle against her.

Tapestry gave a little sigh. *Again?*

"Yes, again," Kate said. "Please."

With a soft grunt, Tapestry dropped to her knees. That was good enough. Making sure her boots were on tight, Kate hoisted one leg over Tapestry's back. She'd never actually tried this before, but she'd seen other riders do it.

"Up," she whispered.

Would it work?

Tapestry hesitated, then lurched to her feet. For a moment Kate worried they'd lose precious seconds if Tapestry decided to shake herself like horses always did when they'd gotten through rolling, but she didn't. So Kate hung onto the ribbons in Tapestry's mane and galloped home to a cheering crowd.

* * *

Angela's winning team slapped her on the back. Gus and Jennifer tried to hoist her into their arms.

Brad stepped in. "Want help?"

"Yikes!" Angela cried, as he lifted her onto his shoulders.

But the grin on Angela's face told Kate that she was loving this. Angela was letting loose and having a grand time—laughing and squealing—and so was everyone else, until their voices dropped to a whisper. Heads turned, someone gasped.

A cloud descended on the group.

In a swirl of black and gray it stalked across the arena like the tornado that blew Dorothy's house from Kansas into Oz—except this time it went in reverse. Colors faded, eyes lost their sparkle, and smiles evaporated.

"Angela," said Mrs. Dean. "What's going on?"

"I'm celebrating."

"Did you win?"

"No, Mother," Angela said waving at her teammates from atop Brad's massive shoulders. "*We* did."

6

"SHE'S A WITCH," HOLLY SAID, after Mrs. Dean hauled Angela from the barn like a cartoon parent dragging a naughty kid by its ear. "She's ruined everything."

"There's still cake," Kate said.

But it didn't feel much like a celebration any more. Mrs. Dean had made sure of that. At least she hadn't reversed her decision to let Kate back into Timber Ridge. She'd just tottered down the aisle in her ridiculous high heels and ordered Angela to come with her. Kate offered to take care of Ragtime.

Angela shrugged. "Whatever."

The barn door had barely closed when Marcia stepped in to help the way she always had with Skywalker. She rubbed Ragtime down, picked out his feet, and fed him even more carrots than she fed Plug.

"Sweet," Holly said.

Liz announced that cake was ready. "Come and get it."

"Yum," Brad said. "I'm totally starving."

"Idiot," said Sue. "You inhaled a whole pizza an hour ago."

"A guy's gotta eat."

Aunt Bea lit all the candles. "Make a wish," she said to Kate like she had earlier at the clinic. Obediently, Kate closed her eyes, but her wish had already come true. She was back at Timber Ridge with her friends.

What else did she want?

She peeked through half-closed eyelids. Dad and Liz were holding hands on the other side of the table, directly behind her birthday cake. It was only a trick of the light, but from this angle they looked like a couple on top of a wedding cake. So Kate made another wish, took a deep breath, and blew out her candles.

Everyone cheered and sang *Happy Birthday*, then dug into the cake. While Gus strummed his guitar, Laura and Marcia sliced up the other carrot cake for the horses.

"Make sure it's the right one," Liz warned.

Despite Marcia's best efforts, Plug managed to get a dab of frosting on his nose. So did Kate.

Brad offered her a napkin. "You want to come skiing tomorrow? The conditions are great." He grinned. "And I promise green trails all the way."

"I can't. I'm sorry," Kate said, "but I'm helping Dad."

"I'll take a rain check," her father said from across the table. "You can work next weekend instead."

"Are you sure?"

Dad relied on her help, and it was part of their bargain. He paid Tapestry's boarding fees at the barn in return for Kate's part-time work at the museum.

Holly nudged her. "We're supposed to be practicing."

"What for?"

"Duh-uh. The Festival of Horses, remember?" She lowered her voice. "We've only got another four weeks."

Kate's mind flew in a dozen directions at once. Besides helping Dad and schooling Tapestry for the show, she had to nail that algebra quiz, get a grip on her homework, and figure out how she really felt about Nathan Crane and Brad Piretti.

But Holly was right.

If they wanted to get noticed by the talent scouts, they needed to practice and practice hard. Magician was in pretty good shape; Tapestry wasn't. Neither was Kate. She'd done precious little riding since leaving the barn last month.

"Do both," Jennifer said.

Sue chimed in. "Ski in the morning and ride in the afternoon."

"Well?" Brad said, looking hopeful.

Kate bit her lip. She couldn't turn him down again, not in front of everyone. It'd be worse than last time.

Why, oh why, hadn't he asked her in private? This was like dating on a television game show.

"Yeah, okay, sure," she said.

It sounded churlish, even to her own ears, but luckily nobody noticed. Well, maybe Brad did, but he was too nice to object. She didn't deserve him. She really didn't. But all this boy girl stuff confused her, especially Nathan's text message that she hadn't read and that now sat in her pocket like a tiny time bomb.

Holly grabbed Adam's hand. "Let's make it a double."

"Date?" he said.

"Why not?"

"Because you don't ski," Kate reminded her. Despite living at Timber Ridge all her life, Holly had never taken skiing lessons. She'd been stuck in a wheelchair for two years and had only gotten back on her feet last summer.

"Pfftt," Holly said, snapping her fingers. "I'll learn."

Jennifer giggled. "How about a triple?"

"Yeah," Gus said. "I'm giving Jen a snowboarding lesson tomorrow. We could all hang out, and—"

A shrill whistle got everyone's attention.

"Okay," Aunt Bea said. "Now that your social issues are sorted, we have one more thing to do." From the depths of her quilted bag, she produced a silver envelope and gave it to Kate. "It's from all of us."

"But you've—"

Kate choked on her words. This was too much . . . over the top. She'd be crying next. For a moment, she just stared at the envelope. It was covered with so many bows and ribbons that it looked as if Aunt Bea had knitted it.

"Go on, open it," Brad said.

Her fingers trembled. "I can't."

"Then I'll help you." Gently, Brad took Kate's envelope, ran his thumb beneath the flap, and popped it open. The card had a dressage horse on the front—a pen-and-ink drawing by Kate's favorite artist—and inside was a gift certificate from Winfield Tack for two hundred dollars.

"Oh," Kate said. "Wow, thank you."

Eyes blurry with tears, she read the signatures—Aunt Bea, Liz, Mr. Evans, Dad, Mrs. Gordon, and all her friends—even Angela's name, written in light blue and barely visible as if she wasn't sure it would be welcome.

Holly thrust a bag at Kate. "For Tapestry."

"Let me open it," Marcia squealed.

Kate was only too happy to oblige. She couldn't handle any more. Nobody had made this much fuss over her birthday since Mom died six years ago. She used to wrap Kate's presents in box after box, each one getting larger, with layers of birthday paper and curly ribbons. It was like digging for buried treasure.

This was Kate's new treasure.

Her friends, her family, and now the fly bonnet that

Marcia was pulling from a nest of blue tissue. The ear parts were black mesh; the front part—the triangle—was a network of intricate black stitches laced together with a touch of silver . . . just like the ones Kate had admired on Olympic grand prix horses. Best of all, it matched Tapestry's fancy browband that Holly had given her last summer.

Kate swallowed hard. "Did you make this?"

"No, Aunt Bea did," Holly said, grinning. "I'm not good enough yet, but I'm working on it."

"Rebel will be totally jealous." Jennifer sighed. "He's been begging me for a designer ear bonnet."

* * *

Leaving Liz to lock up the barn, Kate kissed Tapestry goodnight and followed Holly along the snow-covered path that led to her house. Holly had insisted on a sleepover. She'd also insisted that Kate tell her what was going on with Nathan.

Obviously, she *hadn't* missed his last call.

Kate fingered her cell phone. Half of her didn't want to turn it on, because then she'd have to confront Nathan's latest message. They always left her in a muddle. It was probably nothing more dramatic than *Happy Birthday* with a bunch of smiley faces.

Or it could be full of angst.

The paparazzi lied about his car accident in Palm

Beach; gossip mags were spreading false rumors about him and Tess. And, no, he wasn't drunk or stoned when he showed up for that TV interview in Miami—he had food poisoning.

Arggh, he'd texted. *No more squid!*

Holly said this was normal for celebrities. No matter what they did, someone would blow it out of proportion. Then she reminded Kate that a well-known show jumper had just made equestrian headlines for abusing his horse.

Except he hadn't. It was all a bunch of lies.

Back in the real world of Holly's bedroom, Kate wrapped her hands around a mug of hot chocolate. Stuffed ponies snoozed in a heap on Holly's quilted pillow, show ribbons surrounded both windows, and a herd of wild horses galloped across the ceiling.

"So," Holly said.

Kate looked at her. "What?"

"Nathan," Holly said. "And Brad."

They'd had this conversation before, like a bazillion times, ever since last October when Kate kissed Brad's cheek at the Halloween party.

"I'm thinking," Kate said.

But she wasn't.

She just wanted it all to go away. She wanted someone else to make the decision. Maybe Nathan would quit calling or Brad would back off again. Then she wouldn't have to choose.

"You're a wimp," Holly said.

Kate cringed. "I like them both."

"That's cool," Holly said, "for you, maybe." She took a swig of hot chocolate. "But it's not cool for them. You can't play one against the other."

"I'm not."

"Yes, you are." There was a pause. "You've got a ski date with Brad tomorrow, and next month we're going to the *Moonlight* premiere, remember?" Another pause. "Nathan will expect you to be his date."

"No way," Kate said.

Holly grinned. "Yes, way."

"You're dreaming," Kate said. "He'll have Tess O'Donnell dripping all over him."

Thanks to Holly, she'd watched enough videos on YouTube to know the ropes. Stars hung out with stars; they didn't escort small-town girls across red carpets amid flashbulbs and network cameras, never mind that the movie's director, Giles Ballantine, was sending a car to bring them to New York—Kate and Holly, their parents, and Adam, who'd been Nathan's stunt double in the film.

At this point, Kate wanted the premiere to go away. It was three days before the Festival of Horses and that was far more important. Being in New York the same week and then zooming home to get ready for the show was already stressing her out.

They'd never make it on time.

Something would fall through the cracks and she'd wind up at Long River Horse Park without her dressage saddle or wearing the wrong helmet.

Or worse, without her horse.

"Stop worrying," Holly said. "We'll get you a gorgeous dress and you'll be fabulous. You'll knock everyone's socks off."

That's what Kate was afraid of.

She hated the limelight unless it happened when she was on the back of a horse. Even then, it wasn't easy. And she still hadn't turned on her cell phone. Tomorrow, she'd deal with it tomorrow . . . after she skied with Brad.

Holly thrust a package at her.

"What's this?" Kate said.

"Open it and find out."

Kate tore through brown paper and cardboard to uncover a book. The title said *Turning on a Dime*. It had two girls on the front cover, lots of stars, and a bay horse that looked almost exactly like Ragtime.

"Did he pose for this?" Kate said.

Holly grinned. "It's my new favorite book."

"Better than *Moonlight*?" Kate said.

Holly had raved about that book, and when it got turned into a movie and part of it was shot at Timber Ridge, Holly was in seventh heaven.

"Way better," she declared.

Kate skimmed the back cover—*two girls, from two different centuries, and the horse that brings them together*—then flipped to the first page and read a few paragraphs. Not bad—a teenage rider with attitude and Olympic dreams.

"Thanks," Kate said. "I love it."

"Liar," Holly said, grinning. "But you will. Trust me."

7

LIKE IT HAD ON VALENTINE'S DAY, the mountain erupted with color for St. Patrick's Day. Skiers wearing emerald green hats, mittens, and mufflers carved graceful turns around the lopsided shamrocks that kids had painted in the snow. Rainbows dazzled, balloons bobbed, and lift attendants sported silly green noses.

Kate felt much more confident this time. She left Holly at the bunny hill with a group of beginners, then skied over to join Brad and Adam on the high-speed quad that would take them to the top of Timber Ridge. Jennifer and Gus rode the chair behind them. They would all meet up with Holly at eleven. By then, she'd promised, she would be ready for *Nightmare*.

Kate gave a little shudder.

That was the black diamond run where she'd gotten injured right after Christmas. It almost wrecked her chances to qualify for the Festival of Horses. Inside her thick mittens, Kate crossed her fingers and hoped that Holly wouldn't get hurt. The last thing they needed was another mishap.

The chair slowed and Kate skied off.

Beneath a blanket of deep snow, the mountain's peak was muffled and eerily quiet—well, except for the swoosh and scrape of Gus's snowboard as they followed him down a winding trail toward the half-pipe.

Already a crowd had gathered.

This was Brad's world—extreme snowboarding—but today he was on skis. Kids in baggy clothes gave him high fives; others just stared at their idol. Brad didn't appear to notice the attention.

Gus took a run.

Onlookers cheered as Jennifer's boyfriend swooped and soared and almost zoomed right out of the half-pipe on his razzle-dazzle snowboard.

"You're not gonna do *that*, are you?" Kate said.

Jennifer grinned. "Tomorrow."

Kate didn't doubt it for a minute. Jennifer came from a long line of risk-taking women. Her great-grandmother had ridden sidesaddle over gates and stone walls on the hunt field. Her grandmother, Caroline West, was an Olympic gold medalist and now owned Beaumont Park, one of England's most famous equestrian centers.

Then there was Aunt Judith.

At eighteen, she'd abandoned her British upbringing and run off to America where she joined a rodeo. For nine months she'd toured the mid-West riding broncs, performing back bends and flips on horseback, and jumping mustangs through flaming circles.

Kate couldn't wait to meet her.

With luck, Aunt Judith would be in England when Kate and Holly flew over this summer. They'd been invited to join a special program for talented young riders at Beaumont Park. Much to Mrs. Dean's fury, Angela had not been included.

Moments later Angela skied up with Kristina. They wore matching sherbet outfits—raspberry, mango, and lime.

"The lollypop twins," Jennifer said.

Then came Robin and Sue, followed by Laura and Marcia, armed with food coloring and still drawing shamrocks in the snow. It seemed as if the whole Timber Ridge crowd was out here.

"Next thing," Kate said, "we'll have Liz on skis."

"And Aunt Bea," Robin added.

Kate giggled. "Aunt Bea said that if they ever invented skis like a grown-up tricycle, she'd try it."

"With outriggers," Jennifer said.

Sue laughed. "And a skyhook."

"Sounds like a plan," her brother said. He signaled Kate. "If you're ready, let's go."

Amid whoops and hollers, they left Gus giving Jen her first snowboarding lesson. Kate managed to keep up with Brad along the wide-open trails, but they looked totally different from the grassy slopes she'd ridden last summer with Holly. Rocks and stumps had turned into ice sculptures; snow had obliterated familiar landmarks. Kate took a wrong turn.

Brad skied up and yanked her back.

"Not a good idea," he said, nodding toward a black diamond trail sign that said *Jaws of Death*.

"Whoops."

Heart thumping like sneakers in a dryer, Kate leaned against Brad. Skiers whizzed past. One stopped to ask directions, but Brad waved him on and kept holding Kate as if she were something precious that might fall over if he dared to let go.

"Are you okay?"

"Yes."

He bent down and kissed her.

* * *

Twenty minutes later they met up with Holly on the bunny hill. She snowplowed toward them, arms extended and legs bent inward like a beginner. That's what the bunny hill was all about.

Beginners.

Right now, Kate felt like a beginner in the kissing department. Her cheeks were frozen, her eyelashes frosted with tears, but her lips were still warm where Brad had kissed them.

He'd held her hand, except she hadn't been able to feel it through her bulky mitten. Then he'd said, "I think you're smart and wonderful and pretty." He'd put his finger on her nose. "*Very* pretty."

And then he'd skied off and that was a good thing because otherwise he'd have seen her cry. If Holly noticed her flushed face, she didn't say anything. She just followed everyone down the lower half of the bunny hill and declared she was ready for the next step.

"*Devil's Leap*?" Jennifer said.

Adam grinned. "*Plummet*?"

"Stop teasing," Brad said. "We'll do *Bear Claw*."

It sounded kind of scary to Kate, but it wasn't. Brad took them up the double chair and then led them down a gentle green trail that opened into a panoramic view. He made a spectacular hockey stop and pointed with his ski pole.

"Wow," Holly said. "It's fairyland."

Trees frosted with snow arched over the trail like an old-fashioned bower and framed the valley beyond. Through a filigree of ice, Kate saw red barns and white steeples against a brilliant blue sky—a travel poster for winter in Vermont. Another four weeks from now, it would be spring and she'd be gearing up for the Festival of Horses. She'd also be attending the *Moonlight* pre-miere and seeing Nathan for the first time in seven months.

When they first met, Nathan was a rising star. But Kate, who rarely watched movies, hadn't known who he was until Holly told her. And now, with this film about to be released in New York and all the media hoopla, Nathan Crane had become a glitzy Hollywood sensation.

But had he changed? Like inside?

"Duh-uh," Holly said the previous night. "You bet he has. He's twice as famous, so you'd better put your big girl breeches on."

Trouble was, Kate didn't have any.

All she knew was that *she hadn't* changed. She was still the same girl Nathan met last summer, the girl who preferred paddock boots to party dresses and who'd rather bury herself in the pages of *Dressage Today* and *Chronicle of the Horse* than read a book like *Moonlight*. She glanced at Brad.

"Ready?" he said.

"What for?"

"To leave," he said. "You've got riding practice this afternoon, remember?"

* * *

Nathan's text message was a letdown—just a bunch of smiley faces and *How r u?* Not a word about her birthday. It was like he'd forgotten or had blown it off—or maybe he'd never even gotten Holly's invitation. Reluctantly Kate gave him a pass.

"He's been kinda busy," she said.

Holly snorted. "Yeah, like getting in trouble."

His latest faux pas was telling a reporter that he came from a hick village in Vermont. Nathan's Facebook page had exploded. Half the comments were from fans who didn't even know where Vermont was. But someone called @RebelGirl said: *Dude, your halo just fell off.*

"That sounds like Jen," Holly said.

With a sigh, Kate pocketed her phone. They were in the arena, taking turns at cantering over a line of low jumps without stirrups. Liz kept her riders hard at work—group lessons after school and individual coaching on the weekends.

When the girls weren't practicing half halts, transitions, and leg yielding, they were learning to pace themselves over jumps and studying for the Festival's written test, which Aunt Bea had warned would be rigorous. Nobody was allowed to slack off, not even Sue, Robin, and Kristina, who hadn't qualified for the finals.

"You'll make it next year," Liz said, raising a green-and-white vertical. "So pay attention." She added another layer of blocks to the wall, moved a take-off pole, and then adjusted the spread on a double oxer. "Okay, pick up your stirrups."

Everyone sighed with relief.

Leaning forward, Kate patted Tapestry's neck. She was so comfortable that riding without stirrups was no big deal. But Angela complained that Ragtime's trot was like sitting on a jackhammer.

"Was Skywalker easier?" Kate said, genuinely curious. Ever since Ragtime had unexpectedly taken Skywalker's place, Angela hadn't said a word about her old horse. It was almost as if he'd never existed.

Angela shrugged. "Yeah, kinda, but—"

"Move it," Jennifer said. "It's your turn."

Ragtime flew over the jumps like a seasoned pro. All his rider had to do was sit there looking pretty, and he took care of the rest. *Push-button riding*, Holly called it.

"He's probably memorized the dressage test as well," she said.

Kate gathered up her reins. "Like Magician did?"

At the Hampshire Classic last summer, she'd entered the arena on Holly's horse, trotted down the centerline, and promptly forgot which way to turn. But Magician remembered. After that, the test had come flooding back.

Watching Angela trot toward them, Kate wondered if Ragtime would be better off doing hunter equitation, where correct form over fences was key—not like the rough-and-tumble of cross-country and show jumping, where going fast and clean helped win the blue ribbons at three-day events.

"Well done," Liz called out. "Nice job."

Holly went next.

Magician cleared the course as if it were no more challenging than the toy jumps in Holly's bedroom. He even put in a playful buck at the end.

"Go for it," Holly said, flushed with triumph.

Kate sucked in her breath. "Thanks."

Tapestry jumped the vertical, put in the required three strides, and cleared the brush. Quick turn toward the brick wall. Over and clear. Then came the parallel bars, followed by the combination—a double oxer and another vertical.

They went clean over both.

At the far end, Kate did a rollback and jumped the combination again. They'd be facing similar jumps at the Festival. With luck, it would be held outdoors. It all depended on the weather.

Tomorrow, she and Holly would swap horses. From then on Kate would school Magician because she'd qualified on him for the Festival. She loved Holly's gelding, but part of her wished she could ride her own horse instead.

She knew Holly felt the same way.

* * *

Slowly, the world around Kate began to thaw. Ice dripped off trees, snowdrifts melted into big muddy puddles, and kids at school started throwing baseballs instead of snow-balls. Finally, the riding team was able to practice on the Timber Ridge hunt course.

The horses loved it.

They frisked about like puppies let loose from a cage. Rebel bucked Jennifer off, Cody dumped Kristina, and even Ragtime lost his cool. He shied at a stump and left Angela hanging around his neck. Magician shook his head as if he'd never dream of behaving so badly.

"Good boy," Kate said, laughing.

Rustic fences—rails, log piles, and brush jumps—lay scattered across a wide-open meadow. Three days of sun-shine had softened the ground. Kate took off her hoodie and tied its sleeves around her waist.

"Take it easy," Liz said. "No rushing, okay? It's not a race."

"Tell that to Rebel," Jennifer said. Her gelding was eager to be off and running.

So was Tapestry.

Kate crossed her fingers as Holly and Tapestry ap-proached the first fence. Over they went, then cleared the brush and cantered toward the logs. No problem. Kate's anxiety level dropped another notch. The past month's hard work with Tapestry had paid off.

Then it was her turn with Magician.

He'd jumped this course so many times, he could probably do it with his eyes closed. The only one who hadn't jumped it before was Ragtime, but he handled the fences like he did everything else—efficiently and smoothly, with a little touch of panache.

"Nice," Kate said.

Angela shrugged. "It was okay."

Liz called them into a circle. "This course is about the same difficulty level as the one you'll be riding at Long River, so I don't think you'll have any problems with it," she said. "But the show jumping course will be a challenge."

"Why?" Angela said. "Jumps are jumps."

"It depends on the course designer," Liz replied. "Long River Horse Park is in Connecticut—a maritime state—and I've heard rumors that the stadium jumps will have a nautical theme."

"Does this mean we'll be jumping beach towels and umbrellas?" Jennifer said.

Holly grinned. "Or cute lifeguards?"

"Dream on," Kate said.

＊ ＊ ＊

That night Kate cruised the web for information about Long River. A brand new equestrian facility, the park boasted New England's largest indoor arena, three outside rings, a polo field, four huge barns, and a two-mile cross-country course.

Purring loudly, Persy jumped onto Kate's lap.

"Ouch!" Kate cried.

The cat was almost full grown, but he hadn't yet learned to sheathe his sharp little claws. Kate stroked Persy's shiny black fur, then scooped him into her arms and set him down on her rumpled bed. Her room was a replica of Holly's—pony print comforter, ribbons around the windows, and a bazillion horse posters on the walls.

But the room wasn't hers.

Dad had rented the cottage from his elder sister, Aunt Marion. She'd be back from South Carolina in May to reclaim her house, her rose garden, and her cat. So far, Dad hadn't had any luck finding another place for him and Kate to live.

Not in Winfield, anyway.

"We could always move to Rutland," he'd said.

Kate tried not to complain, but it would mean a whole new school and being even further away from her friends and Timber Ridge.

Holly remained optimistic. "When our parents—"

"*If*," Kate corrected.

"Okay, *if* our parents get married," Holly went on, "you can live at my house."

Except it wasn't Holly's house.

It belonged to the Timber Ridge Homeowners' Association, and it went with Liz's job. Kate had stayed with the Chapmans last summer while her dad was on a field trip in Brazil. But when he returned in late October and they moved into Aunt Marion's cottage, Mrs. Dean had promptly kicked Kate off the riding team.

"It's for residents only," she'd declared.

But if Kate wound up living at Timber Ridge again, she'd be eligible for the team—and who knew what horrors Mrs. Dean would dream up to keep her off it.

Holly predicted rats. "Like the Pied Piper."

"Black flies," Jennifer said, "big as jumbo jets."

"Never-ending mud season," Sue said. "From now until forever."

Kate took it all in good fun, but deep down she knew that Mrs. Dean would do anything—anything at all—to keep her off the riding team so that Angela could be its superstar. It made absolutely no sense. Holly and Jennifer were brilliant riders—better than Angela—but Mrs. Dean hadn't targeted them with her venom.

Just Kate.

8

A WEEK BEFORE THE *MOONLIGHT* PREMIERE, Holly cornered Kate in her bedroom and announced that they really needed to get new dresses.

"Why can't I wear this?" Kate said.

From Holly's closet she pulled out the slinky red gown she'd bought at the thrift shop for the school's Valentine dance, except she'd never worn it.

But Holly had.

It was right after her fight with Kate. They weren't speaking to each other, and Holly had wanted to strike out. So she'd worn Kate's dress to the dance instead of her own. She still felt guilty about it.

"Because this is a really big deal," Holly said. "There'll be TV cameras and Hollywood reporters, stars in tiaras and fur coats, and—"

"Fur?" Kate shrieked. "*Real* fur?"

"Fake," Holly said.

But was it? Nobody could tell these days. The diamonds and gold were probably fake, too, but they glittered and that was all that mattered to the legions of fans who'd be shrieking over Nathan Crane and Tess O'Donnell.

Holly thought for a minute.

Two girls from a tiny village in Vermont couldn't compete with all that, but one thing they could do was hit the fancy boutique that Angela was always blathering about.

"Let's go to Blaines."

"Get real," Kate said. "We can't afford it."

"Mr. Ballantine's studio is paying," Holly reminded her. "For you, me, and Mom. They want us to look good."

"What about Dad and Adam?" Kate said.

"White tie and tails," Holly replied, "from Rent-a-Tux."

"So why can't we do the same?"

"Because women don't rent dresses," Holly said and shoved Kate out the door where Mom was waiting with the van to take them into Winfield.

"How long will you need?" Liz said.

"Ten minutes," Kate replied.

Holly rolled her eyes. "All afternoon."

They settled on two hours. It wouldn't be nearly

enough, but it was better than nothing. Kate could spend all day in a tack shop obsessing over just the right stirrup leathers, but when it came to clothes and shoes, she had the attention span of a dressage rider at a rodeo.

* * *

The saleslady, whose name tag said *Janice*, fussed and fluttered like a giant moth. She produced an endless stream of fluffy prom dresses and elaborate bridesmaids' gowns until Kate was ready to scream.

"Graduation," Holly said.

Kate grimaced. "Weddings."

"Don't knock it," Holly said. "I want Mom here next month choosing her—"

"How about this?" Janice said.

The dress was a deep, iridescent blue with a long, swirly skirt, a scooped neckline, and tiny cap sleeves. Silver stars twinkled on its matching gauzy stole.

"Perfect," Holly said. "Try it on."

Moments later, Kate turned slowly in front of the three-way mirror. Despite her striped socks and messy hair, she looked kind of good. More than good. Maybe it was an illusion. She peered closer as Holly stuck her head into the fitting room.

"Awesome," she said.

Eyes glinting like dollar signs, Janice draped the stole around Kate's shoulders. "It's totally you," she gushed.

Kate didn't dare look at the price tag.

This dress probably cost more than a custom-made saddle. But, as Holly kept reminding her, Giles Ballantine could afford it. Last summer, he'd dropped a small fortune on a high-spirited horse named Buccaneer, brought him to Timber Ridge for a month's training, and then moved him on after the filming was over.

Nobody knew where Buccaneer went.

Holly tried on a dozen different outfits, but in the end, she came back to her first choice—a rose pink gown with skinny straps, a silver sash, and a bias-cut skirt that even Kate had to agree was absolutely perfect. Janice added the finishing touches—silver sandals and a pink puffball shrug trimmed with tiny silver beads.

"You're a princess," Kate said.

Holly struck a pose. "Watch out, Ophelia Brown."

"Who?"

"The girl in *Moonlight*," Holly said, with a dramatic sigh. "Haven't you read the book yet?"

Kate nodded, even though she'd never finished it. "I just forgot her name."

"How could you?" Holly teased. "You played her in the movie."

"I didn't," Kate said. "Tess O'Donnell did."

"But you did the hard part," Holly said. "You rode that scene bareback, remember?"

"Yeah," Kate said, grinning. "I'm still sore."

She'd only done it to earn money for a horse. Otherwise she had zero interest in movies. That was Holly's department. She loved the glitz and the glamour, and it should've been her riding Magician, not Kate. But Holly's legs weren't strong enough last summer, so she'd sat on the sidelines while Kate had ridden Magician through the woods and over fences without a saddle until Giles Ballantine said, "Cut!"

"Aren't you excited about New York?" Holly said, as Janice wrapped their dresses in gold tissue.

"Huh?"

"You and Magician," Holly said. "On the big screen."

"Screen?" Janice looked up. "Like in a movie?"

"Oh, yes," Holly said, with a perfectly straight face. "Didn't you know that Kate McGregor is a famous film star?"

* * *

Still giggling, they scurried out of Blaines and bumped into Angela, arm-in-arm with her cousin Courtney. Beneath their white snowflake vests, both girls wore white cableknit sweaters, creamy white ski pants, and white mukluks that had so much fur they reminded Kate of the Budweiser horses' feathery fetlocks.

"My little snow ponies," Holly said.

Courtney raised a well-plucked blond eyebrow and stared at Kate's distinctive black-and-gold shopping bag as if she couldn't believe it.

"Blaines?" she said. "You have *got* to be kidding."

"They're faking it," Angela said reaching for Holly's bag. "I bet there's a thrift shop disaster in here."

"Wrong," Holly snapped.

Kate tugged at her arm. "C'mon," she said. "Your mom will be waiting."

Clearly, Angela's patience at being halfway decent had run out. She was back to her old self. In a weird sort of way, it was almost comforting, as if the other shoe had dropped and Kate could stop worrying about it landing on her head.

Liz's van pulled up to the curb.

Leaning out the window, she waved at Angela and Courtney. "Do you girls need a ride home?"

"No," Angela said, and sauntered off.

"Bratface," Holly muttered, throwing herself into the van's front seat. "She never even said thank you."

*   *   *

The weekend zoomed by in a whirlwind of riding lessons, cleaning tack, and studying for the Festival's written test. Every muscle in Kate's body ached as she forced her brain to wrap itself around the difference between *founder* and *laminitis*.

"What's a *grulla*?" Holly said.

Jennifer sighed. "Look it up."

"Big help you are," Holly grumbled.

They'd invited Angela to join their last-minute cram

session, but she had refused. "I know all that stuff," she'd said.

Kate couldn't take her mind off the premiere.

Mr. Ballantine's assistant had called. The studio's limo would pick them up at nine on Tuesday morning. They'd be in New York by early afternoon. The premiere was at seven thirty, with a reception to follow at the Regency Hotel. On Wednesday, they'd be driven back to Vermont in time to pack up their horses and head for Long River Park on Thursday . . . if nothing went wrong.

What if there was bad weather or a lame horse? Or suppose the limo broke down and they—

Holly gave an exasperated sigh. "Chill out."

But the more Kate tried to relax, the worse she got. Not about the show—Magician was a dream to ride—but about Nathan. She didn't dare admit it in front of Holly, but she was scared to death of seeing him again especially after Sunday night's fiasco.

It was all over Facebook.

Nathan, still recognizable despite oversized sunglasses and a cowboy hat, was being dragged—the article said "helped"—by his bodyguard from a New York nightclub.

Food poisoning? Again?

"I can't chill," Kate said.

"Then fake it," Holly said. "Because you're driving me nuts."

* * *

On Tuesday morning, Aunt Bea and Mr. Evans took charge of the barn. along with Jennifer, Sue, and Robin as their willing assistants. Angela had flown to the Bahamas for three days and would meet them at the Festival in Connecticut.

"Typical," Holly said.

Trust Angela to dump her chores on everyone else. It would be tough enough to get their own horses ready for the show, never mind having to take care of Ragtime, too, even if he was a total sweetheart.

Adam squeezed her hand. "We'll manage."

He'd trucked Domino over the night before and would be traveling with them to Long River because nobody else from his barn had qualified. So that meant five horses in the Timber Ridge van. It held six, but with all their gear for three days, plus hay and—

The limo pulled up—long and black, with tinted windows and more chrome than Mr. Evans's outrageous Cadillac that had steer horns on the front bumper.

Holly rubbed her eyes. "Is this for real?"

"It's our getaway car," Adam said, grinning.

The driver, wearing a white suit, aviator shades, and black gloves, hefted their suitcases into the limo's capacious trunk. Then he opened the rear doors and Holly gasped—wrap-around sofas, plasma screen TV, and softly glowing lights that reminded her of a starship's flight deck. She pulled off her pink baseball cap.

"Guess I should've worn the tiara, huh?"

Mom smiled, then helped herself to a bottle of Evian water from the mini-fridge and settled into a plush leather seat beside Kate's dad. Holly couldn't be sure, but were they holding hands? She nudged Kate, but her best friend was too busy staring out the window.

* * *

Vermont slid by, then Massachusetts, and in no time they were cruising toward the New York City skyline. Adam whistled through his teeth.

"Watch out, Manhattan. Here we come."

Then came a serious traffic jam on the Upper West Side and it was almost four o'clock when they drove beneath the Regency Hotel's purple awnings on Park Avenue. Doormen in purple livery opened the limo's doors.

"Hair first," Holly said, striding into the hotel's opulent foyer as if she owned it. "Then nails and face."

Before Kate had a chance to object, she found herself being guided toward a salon with recessed lights, soft music, and smiling beauticians. She landed in a plush swivel chair. Someone wrapped fluffy towels around her neck.

Did Holly engineer this?

"Don't fight it," Liz said from the chair beside Kate.

Warm water flowed; gentle fingers massaged fragrant

shampoo into Kate's scalp. She sighed and gave up. She'd probably end up with more makeup than Lady Gaga and hair like a plastic mermaid, but if it made Holly happy, she'd go along with it. Besides, it took her mind off Nathan.

Can't wait 2 c u, said his last text.

Kate wasn't sure she believed him.

* * *

Holding Dad's arm, Liz emerged from the elevator barely recognizable in a long black dress that shimmered as she walked toward them. Diamond studs glittered in Liz's ears; her blond hair glowed with highlights. Kate sucked in her breath. She'd never seen Holly's mom like this before. From the way Dad was hovering, he hadn't either.

"You nailed it, Mom," Holly said, proudly.

Kate smoothed her skirt, then tugged at her gauzy blue wrap. It was starting to feel worse than hay when it got stuck inside your socks. "It itches."

"Get over it," Holly muttered.

Already Kate's toes were complaining. She shouldn't have worn the wedge heels Holly had insisted on. Good thing she'd shoved a pair of flats into her knapsack.

"You can't bring *that* into a movie premiere," Holly warned.

With a flourish, Adam flipped the tails of his dinner jacket. "I'm a grand prix dressage rider."

"More like a head waiter," Holly said.

"That's *my* job," Dad said. "Is my tie on straight?"

He looked so anxious that Kate wanted to hug him. Dad wasn't used to fancy clothes any more than she was. At the butterfly museum he hung around in faded cords, deck shoes, and cardigans with leather patches on the elbows. But right now, he really did look great—distinguished, even.

"It's fine, Ben," Liz said, patting his arm.

Holly rolled her eyes at Kate and mouthed, *Like an old married couple.*

Their limo arrived. Adam cupped Holly's elbow and guided her into the back seat. Kate climbed in behind them and sat between Liz and Dad.

He patted Kate's knee. "Excited?"

"Kinda."

No, make that nervous and about to freak out.

Like a sleek black panther, the limo purred toward Broadway. Neon signs blinked; horns blared. Yellow cabs changed lanes faster than a video game. When they glided to a stop at the movie theater, fans screamed and banged on the limo's tinted windows. Kate wanted to curl up and die.

"Wow," Holly said. "This is wicked cool."

In a blitz of flashbulbs, she hammed it up for the media who stuck microphones in her face, then turned away disappointed when they didn't recognize her name.

But Holly didn't care. Linking arms with Adam, she just laughed as the frenzied reporters pounced on their next victim. Whoever climbed out of a limo was fair game.

Paparazzi shoved and pushed.

One punched a rival in the face, busted his camera, and got hauled off by the police. Another limo rolled up—sparklingly white with gold hubcaps and tiny gold flags on its hood. Uniformed men opened doors. More lights went off. A hush descended over the crowd.

Who was it this time?

Then cheers erupted as Tess O'Donnell, swathed in a cloud of billowing white chiffon, emerged from her gilded coach like a Disney princess.

The fans went wild.

As if on cue, a gentle breeze lifted Tess's golden curls and blew delicate tendrils around her glowing face. She smiled and posed for the camera. Her blue eyes skimmed over Kate and Holly as if she didn't recognize them.

"He's here!" someone yelled.

Nathan?

Kate turned and almost tripped over a tasseled red rope. It cordoned off the important from the not so important. One of the theater's ushers pulled her to one side, behind the rope. Kate stood on tiptoe, but she couldn't see over the crush of people. Men with slicked-back hair and ruffled shirts got in her way; a woman wearing diamonds, feathers, and four-inch heels trod on Kate's foot.

A murmur ran through the crowd.

Excited shouts rang out. The murmur grew into a roar. Frantically, Kate looked around for Holly and Adam, but they'd been swept into the mass of people along with Dad and Liz.

"Keep moving, please," said an usher.

Two more ushers with outstretched arms guided everyone deeper into the theater's luxurious lobby. "Let's clear the carpet, folks."

Kate shoved as hard as she could and burst to the front in time to see Nathan with his back toward her, arm draped around Tess's shoulders and waving to a surging mob of fans. Flashbulbs dazzled, reporters yelled, and TV cameras hummed.

Someone called for a different angle.

Nathan turned and, for an instant, the dark glasses he wore slipped down his nose. He shoved them back up, but not before Kate caught a glimpse of bloodshot eyes.

9

"ARE YOU OKAY?" HOLLY SAID. They were in the theater, front-row balcony, with a terrific view of the celebrities below. Last-minute arrivals, including Nathan and Giles Ballantine, hurried to their seats.

"Yes." Kate hesitated. "No."

"Hang in there," Holly said.

She knew Kate was sweating this—not like you did before a horse show when all your friends were going through exactly the same fears and anxiety, but about seeing Nathan again.

Down went the lights.

Up came the music and swept them into the world of *Moonlight*. Vampires sparkled, horses flew, and were-wolves prowled. Kate's scene was almost at the end, when thugs on motorcycles chased Ophelia Brown through the woods. Wearing jeans and a blue t-shirt, the heroine galloped down narrow trails and over impossible jumps, then got sucked into a time portal and emerged on the other side in a flowing white dress.

The motorcycles morphed into zombies.

Blood dripping from teeth and eyeballs, they tore after Ophelia, getting closer and closer until the movie's golden hero, Ian Hamilton, galloped up and rescued her.

The audience cheered. "Go, Tess."

"Idiots," Holly muttered.

They had no clue that it wasn't Tess riding Magician or that Adam was doubling for Nathan.

The party afterward was just as bad. People swarmed around Tess O'Donnell, gushing words of meaningless praise about how brave she was to ride a horse like that.

"Weren't you scared?" said a girl with pouty lips.

"Oh, no," Tess said, posing yet again for the cameras. "It was amazing fun. I just adore horses. They're so"— she flashed an award-winning smile—"soft and furry."

"Phony," Holly muttered to Kate.

Last summer it had taken every ounce of patience they possessed to get the terrified Tess O'Donnell onto Magician for her one big close-up. She'd been super grateful for the help, but now, here she was, showing off and pretending to have ridden the scene bareback all by herself.

"It's okay," Kate said. "I don't mind."

But Holly did. She wanted to strangle Tess O'Donnell with the floaty white scarves that hung from her selfish shoulders. Instead, she mentally struck Tess off her list of favorite stars and checked the door again. No sign of Nathan. He was probably running late on purpose so he could make a grand entrance.

Holly glanced at Adam. With his green eyes and streaky blond hair, he looked so much like Nathan that several party guests had asked for his autograph. Right now, he was chatting up a couple of star-struck grand-mothers.

He turned and winked at Holly.

She winked back. Earlier they'd talked about Nathan because Adam was worried that his friend had changed.

For once, Holly had kept her mouth shut.

She knew Nathan had changed, but she didn't want to burst Adam's bubble. He probably didn't know that his best buddy had badmouthed their home town yet again. It was all over YouTube yesterday morning.

"Where did you grow up?" a reporter had asked.

Nathan had brushed him off. "No place special. Just a backwater in Vermont."

From a passing waiter, Holly scooped up two cheese pastries, a handful of spiced nuts, and something on a stick that looked suspiciously like fried broccoli.

"Here," she said to Kate. "Have a veggie."

"Not hungry."

Holly sighed. Across the huge ballroom she spotted Giles Ballantine heading toward them. Maybe he'd know where Nathan was.

* * *

"Hello, ladies," the director said. "Having a good time? What did you think of the film?"

"Awesome," Holly said, "and Kate—"

"She was awesome, too," Mr. Ballantine said. He scooped Kate into a one-armed hug that almost knocked the breath out of her. "And what about my boy, heh? Didn't he do a fine job? I told everyone he'd be a big star, and—"

"Where is—?" Holly said.

"Buccaneer," Kate blurted.

It slipped out, just like that. She hadn't meant it to, but it was less awkward than asking about Nathan. Plus she really wanted to find out where Buccaneer had gone. He'd been a big part of her life until he dropped off everyone's radar once the filming was over last summer. Mr. Ballantine looked kind of confused, as if he couldn't place the name. "Oh, you mean my horse?"

"Yes," Kate said.

"We sold him in October."

Holly stepped in. "Who to?"

"I don't remember." Giles Ballantine drained his glass of champagne, then snagged another. "My manager took care of it."

Kate was about to push when Holly squeezed her arm. "Not now," she whispered.

"Why?"

"Because Nathan's here."

Kate felt herself turning inside out. She ran hot and cold. This was far worse than waiting your turn to ride a dressage test or tackle cross-country jumps with names like Tiger's Trap and Witch's Broomstick.

Wearing an open-necked shirt beneath his tuxedo, Nathan sauntered into the room with his arms draped around a giggling redhead and a blonde whose makeup looked as if it had been slathered on with a putty knife. Was one of these Yolanda Quinn, the *Moonlight* author? Nathan had promised to introduce them.

He looked at Kate. "Hello, babe."

Babe?

He'd called her that once before, and his well-known voice had ricocheted around the barn because she'd left her speakerphone on by mistake. But not this time. She wouldn't let him get away with it. Something inside her snapped.

She was so over this.

"I am *not* your babe, Nathan Crane."

The room went silent. Conversation died, waiters halted in mid-stride, and all eyes turned toward Kate. Seeing him like this had broken the spell. Nathan was just an ordinary guy who'd gotten blindsided by Hollywood and was stupid enough to believe in his own publicity. Video cameras appeared; flashbulbs fired.

But Kate didn't flinch.

Who cared if she wound up on YouTube or Facebook or plastered on the front page of Nathan's silly fan magazines? This was nothing more than a flash in the pan. Tonight she was the girl from nowhere who snubbed Nathan Crane; tomorrow she'd be old news and the gossip monkeys would find something else to twitter about.

"C'mon," she said to Holly. "I'm outta here."

"Wait," Holly said, rounding on Nathan. "You said Yolanda Quinn was coming. Where is she?"

"Dunno." He shrugged. "I guess she couldn't make it."

Somewhere in the depths of Kate's beaded purse, her cell phone rang. She checked caller ID, then turned on the speakerphone at full blast. "Hello."

"Hi, Kate," said Brad. "How's it going?"

* * *

Still talking to Brad, Kate rode the elevator with Holly up to their bedroom. Holly nudged her.

Are you okay? she mouthed.

With a quick nod, Kate switched her phone from one ear to the other. All these months of pretending that Nathan really cared about her vanished like bubbles in a bathtub.

"I brushed Tapestry," Brad said. "She misses you."

Kate caught her breath. "Thanks."

"And tell Holly that Aunt Bea called the farrier," he went on. "One of Magician's shoes is loose."

After more thanks and a promise to call in the morning, Kate rang off. "Wow."

"Nice guy?"

"I didn't realize." Kate sat down hard on the bed.

Holly sat beside her. "Been telling you," she said. "Brad's a keeper. Nathan Crane isn't."

"I feel bad for Adam," Kate said. "Nathan's his best friend."

"They'll figure it out."

"How?"

"Guys live on another planet," Holly said. "Didn't you know that?"

"No."

"But girls live on a better planet," Holly went on. "And sometimes we let the guys in, but only if they wise up and play by our rules."

Kate pursed her lips. "Yeah, right."

"No, really," Holly said. "It happens."

"Like when?"

"When we teach them," Holly said. "But they don't always get it." She paused. "It really helps if the guy likes horses. You can't be a jerk around the barn because horses can sniff out jerks faster than—"

"—Magician gobbles up carrots?"

Holly grinned. "You got it."

* * *

The next morning, they met Marcia Dean and her father in the hotel foyer. He took them on a whirlwind tour of Lower Manhattan, a breathtaking trip up the Empire State Building, and lunch at a roadside cart in Central Park that sold the best hot dogs Kate had ever tasted.

Dad got mustard all over his beard.

Gently, Liz wiped it off with a napkin and chided him for being sloppy.

Holly nudged Kate. "See?"

The limo picked them up at two thirty, and by seven they were back at the barn. Kate raced inside, smothered Tapestry with kisses, and then hugged Aunt Bea. "Thanks for everything."

"What about me?" Brad said.

Kate froze.

"Go on," Holly said, giving her a gentle push.

Caught off balance, Kate landed in Brad's arms. It was like being hugged by a teddy bear. She felt herself relax, the way she had when Brad hugged her on the mountain. Was he going to kiss her again, in front of everyone? Adam let out a low whistle.

"How was the premiere?" Aunt Bea said.

"Awesome," said Adam, puffing out his chest. "I signed three autographs."

"Show off," Holly said.

Kate bit her lip, hoping Aunt Bea wouldn't ask about

Nathan. Last summer she'd taken quite a shine to him. They all had, because back then he was a likable guy. Angela had been all over him like sparkles on a vampire. She'd pestered Nathan for his cell number and had been totally incensed when he'd given it to Kate instead.

"Kate?" Aunt Bea said. "Are you all right?"

"Yes," Kate said. "Just a little nervous."

"About the show?"

"Yeah," Holly said, rolling her eyes. "It's only the biggest one of the year."

"You'll do fine," Aunt Bea said. "Just remember that trying your best and feeling good about yourself are more important than winning prizes."

Tears pricked at Kate's eyelids.

This was exactly what her mother used to say. Had Aunt Bea been swapping notes with Dad? Did he even remember what Mom said every time she took Kate to a horse show?

Dad rarely came with them. He was either off chasing butterflies or squirreled away in his office writing another book. And when he did come to shows, he was more interested in the bot flies that laid tiny orange eggs on the horses' legs than in Kate's riding.

It got worse after Mom died. Dad pulled into his shell like a turtle and didn't come out until they moved to Vermont. Falling for Liz was the best thing that had happened to him. At least, Kate hoped he was falling. It sure looked like it. They'd spent the whole trip home in the limo holding hands.

Just before they left the barn, Brad dropped a kiss on Kate's cheek. "For luck," he whispered.

She blushed. "Thanks."

From the corner of her eye, Kate saw Holly giving her a thumbs-up.

* * *

With Liz at the wheel and Kate beside her, they hit the road at seven. Brad had helped load the van and promised to be at the show on Saturday.

"To cheer you on," he'd told Kate.

"And me?" Holly said.

Brad grinned. "You've got Adam."

"Duh-uh," Holly said. "He rides for another team."

But this time it didn't matter, Kate realized, as they rolled south toward Connecticut. They were riding as individuals, not as a team. Surprisingly Mrs. Dean didn't seem to care. Her goal was to make sure that Angela got noticed by talent scouts from the United States Equestrian Federation.

"Maybe Angela will ride in a bikini," Holly said from the back seat. "That would get their attention."

"And mine," Adam said.

Kate turned around. "Did you guys pack bathing suits?"

"Are you nuts?" Holly said, zipping up her hoodie. "It's still winter out there."

"Not in Connecticut," Kate said. "I went to the beach during spring break two years ago."

"And last year you were shoveling snow," Holly reminded her.

Adam plucked at the white track shorts he wore over his sweatpants. "I'm covered both ways."

"I'm not," Holly said, pouting.

"So, borrow Angela's bikini," Adam said.

Holly pulled a face. "Blecchh."

* * *

Dozens of trucks, vans, and trailers waited their turn to pass through the security gates at Long River Horse Park. Roads forked in different directions and white signposts pointed toward barns with names like *Mark Twain, Nutmeg,* and *Charter Oak.*

Liz checked her paperwork. "We're stabled in *Mountain Laurel.*"

"What's that?" Adam said.

"Connecticut's state flower," Kate replied, "like Vermont's is red clover."

"Smarty-pants," Holly said, grinning.

The sun broke through a bank of clouds. Kate lowered her window, and fresh air wafted into the van. They were only ten miles from the ocean, and Kate pretended she could smell it; if she tried hard enough, she could hear seagulls, too.

That was the one thing she missed living in Vermont—being able to ride a horse along the beach. She'd done it once with Black Magic at her old stable and had never forgotten the amazing sensation of being on his back while he swam. He'd even jumped the waves. Kate had laughed so hard that she'd fallen off.

She glanced in the van's side mirror. Behind them, Jennifer waved from her mother's Range Rover. Kate waved back.

"Looks like the jumping will be outside," Liz said.

In a show ring the size of a football field, officials were pacing off distances. A flatbed truck piled with rails, flower boxes, and colorful side wings trundled around. In the center of the ring was a lifeguard's stand shaded by a red beach umbrella.

Holly pouted. "So, where's the cute lifeguard?"

"Right here," Adam said. "If you fall into the Liverpool, I'll dive in and save you."

Liz jerked the wheel to avoid a Jack Russell terrier that darted across the road. Its owner was too busy talking with a friend to notice.

"Stupid dogs," Holly said.

"No," said her mother. "Stupid people."

Along one side of the show ring, red-and-blue flags fluttered from hospitality tents like pennants at a yacht club. Inside were buffet tables and comfortable seats for people who were important enough to be invited. Red ropes hung across the openings.

"To keep out the riff-raff," Holly said. "Like us."

Despite Mrs. Dean's best efforts, Timber Ridge didn't have a hospitality tent this year. No doubt Angela's mother would bulldoze her way into another members-only tent, like Spruce Hill or Fox Meadow Hunt Club.

Kate glanced at the rows of padded bleachers on the ring's opposite side. They were much fancier than the ones at school—more like a small grandstand. Brad would be impressed.

Slowly, they drove past a line of vendors and food carts with dark green awnings that sold everything from lattes and cappuccino muffins to Hermes saddles, Ariat boots, and diamond-studded baseball hats.

Holly's head was on a swivel. "Shopping!"

"You're broke, remember?" Kate said.

"Spoilsport."

Liz pulled into the Mountain Laurel parking lot. "I'll drop you kids here," she said. "Then I'll hit the show secretary's booth for numbers and a schedule."

Skinny fir trees in wooden tubs flanked the barn's main entrance. No sign of any mountain laurels, which was a good thing. They were poisonous to horses. Dogs, too, probably.

"What comes first?" Kate said.

"The written test," Liz said as she maneuvered her van into a space near the door. "And judging for stable management is going on all the time, so—"

"—pick up your stall every five seconds," Holly said, then whispered to Kate, "and watch out for Angela."

Kate gave a little shudder. At the Hampshire Classic last year Angela had trashed Magician's stall moments before the judges came by. The Timber Ridge team lost valuable points and so did Kate, which was part of Angela's nasty plan. She didn't care about their team, just about winning the individual gold medal.

The stakes were even higher this time.

10

WEARING SPOTLESS WHITE BREECHES and a Caribbean tan, Angela sauntered into the written test five seconds before the door closed. She looked around, then chose a seat near the window.

"Grand entrance again," Holly said.

They sat at wooden desks in rows. It was like being in middle school, but without a blackboard and diagrams of frogs on the wall. Holly did a quick head count. Fifty-seven kids in the novice division. The advanced riders would take their test later.

Holly looked at hers.

Question one: *A horse's stifle is equivalent to a human's ankle, knee, toe, or elbow?*

Picturing a horse's skeleton, Holly opted for *knee*.

Question two: *Where are the ergots found?*

Easy peasy. *Back of fetlock.*

Holly checked the box and glanced at Kate. Her head was down and she was busy writing. It looked as if she'd almost filled in the first page. Two rows further back, Jennifer grinned and gave Holly a thumbs-up.

They'd all been drilled and quizzed by Aunt Bea, even Angela, although she probably hadn't paid attention. Right now, she was staring out the window as if the written test didn't matter. Maybe Mrs. Dean had bribed the officials to give Angela a pass, no matter what.

The test took an hour and Holly felt wrung out at the end of it, just as if she'd jumped the cross-country course without her stirrups. As soon as they were out the door, she grabbed Kate. "Who won the first triple crown?"

Jennifer groaned. "As if it matters."

"Seabiscuit?" Kate said.

Angela pushed past them. "Sir Barton."

Holly whipped out her cell phone and punched up the answer. "Yikes. How did she know that?"

* * *

The dressage phase began at eight on Friday morning. Unlike other three-day events, these were all freestyle tests, with riders choosing the movements that best suited them and their horses.

Mentally, Kate ran over the rules again.

The Festival had its own scoring system, and you even got to talk to the judge for a few minutes after your test. Kate's was at twelve thirty, right before the lunch break.

Was this good or bad?

"It's perfect," Holly said, rolling her eyes. "The judges will be so delirious with hunger they'll give you a perfect score."

"Why?"

"So they can bolt into the food tent."

Kate giggled. "Dream on."

Perfect scores were impossible. They sometimes happened in gymnastics and figure skating, but not in dressage. Even Kate's favorite Olympic grand prix rider, Ineke Van Klees, had never scored above eighty-one percent.

Holly went first, and Kate bit her lip as Tapestry trotted into the indoor arena. It wasn't really an indoor; more like a coliseum, but larger than the one in Springfield where they'd gone to see the *Equine Affaire* last November.

But she needn't have worried.

Holly and Tapestry aced their test like a couple of pros. They sailed through half passes, extended trots, and a shoulder-in as if they'd been doing this routine forever. The audience clapped. They didn't know that Holly had only been riding Tapestry for a month.

Sixty-eight, said the scoreboard.

Kate punched the air with her fist. "Whoopee."

If Magician did this well, she would be over the moon.

Another hour. Almost time to get ready. Holly's horse whickered as she entered his stall. Had he rubbed out his braids?

No, thank goodness.

"Good boy," she said, counting them—fifteen knobby little topknots that ran down the crest of his neck. Holly had done a great job on him, while Kate had given Tapestry a running French braid because her mane was too long and thick to braid like Magician's.

Quickly, Kate mucked out Magician's stall, refilled his water bucket, and knocked down a stray cobweb. Had the stable management judges been by yet? Earlier that morning, she'd heard two girls grumbling about this part of the competition.

"We have grooms for this," one said.

The other chimed in, "Our trainer won't even let us saddle our horses."

"So," Holly said, as if butter wouldn't melt in her mouth, "why are you here?"

Two pairs of hostile eyes glared at her.

"Peasant," the first girl said.

"No, I'm Riffraff," Holly said, then pointed her pitchfork at Kate. "That's Peasant."

Grinning to herself, Kate now stripped off Magician's blanket, gave him a quick brush, and saddled him up. It was hard to believe that some kids didn't know how to do this, or to pick out a horse's hoof, or—

"Good luck," said a familiar voice.

Kate whipped around so fast she almost fell over. "Oh, hi."

"Be careful." Lockie Malone grinned at her. "Don't mess up that knee again."

Wow, he remembered.

"I won't."

"This isn't your horse, is it?" he said.

Holly was still outside with Tapestry, cooling her down. "No," Kate said. "Magician belongs to my best friend."

"Ah," he said. "Now I remember. You guys switched horses for this show."

Kate brought Magician into the aisle. "Yes."

"Need a leg-up?"

For a mad moment, Kate was tempted to show off by vaulting into the saddle, which she often did—not always successfully. More than once she'd missed and landed, with great embarrassment, on her butt.

She gathered up her reins. "Thanks."

"Ready?" he said.

Kate nodded, then lifted her knee, and Lockie Malone hoisted her on board as if she weighed no more than a flake of hay.

"Good bone," he said, patting Magician's shoulder. "I bet he's strong on the cross-country course."

"Very," Kate said. "Like a train."

"Well, good luck," Lockie said again, then stuck both

hands in his pockets and sauntered down the aisle, whistling off-key as he turned a corner and disappeared.

Holly led Tapestry into the barn.

"I love, *love*, your horse," she said to Kate and flung her arms around Tapestry's neck. "She's the best. Did you see that cracking half pass we made?"

"Hush," Kate said leaning forward to cover Magician's ears. "He's gonna be jealous."

"Nah," Holly said. "He's too cool for that."

Kate laughed and then rode out of the barn to warm up in the practice ring. Trotting along the rail, she lowered her hands and sat deep in the saddle. Magician flicked his ears, then responded the way he always did. It wasn't the same as riding Tapestry, but it was a very close second best.

As soon as Magician was warmed up, Kate put him through their routine twice and hoped he'd pull off his flying change without a hitch in front of the judges. It was a bit of a gamble—impressive to watch, but tough to do.

Kate cantered another circle: *Inside leg on the girth; outside leg behind it. Cross the centerline, swap leg positions. Bend the horse through its entire body. Keep hands gentle. Make it look like you're not doing anything at all.*

Magician broke into a trot.

Not good.

If they did this in the ring, they'd be faulted. Kate was

about to try again when Liz waved from the arena's main entrance.

"Five minutes." She ducked back inside.

Kate patted Magician's neck. "No matter what happens," she whispered, "you're a rock star."

They reached the arena's warm-up ring in time to see the last half of Angela's performance. Nose almost vertical, Ragtime floated across the tanbark with hooves that barely seemed to touch the ground.

Then came a fumble, and another.

Ragtime righted himself, but it would cost Angela precious points. Moments later, her mouth was a thin line as she left the ring with a score of sixty-one percent. Not bad, considering her mistakes, but Mrs. Dean obviously didn't see it that way.

Eyes blazing, she met Angela at the gate. "That was unacceptable. I paid a fortune for this horse, and—"

Kate wanted to cover her ears. She hated overhearing this, but the warm-up ring was small and Mrs. Dean's voice carried like a foghorn. Everyone heard, including Liz and the other trainer she'd been talking to.

Would Angela defend herself?

You never knew. Sometimes she blasted her mother right back; at other times she hid behind a mask of indifference.

Liz interrupted. "She did fine, Viola."

"Not in my book," Mrs. Dean snapped.

She took a step toward Ragtime, but her heel caught on a chunk of tanbark and only Liz's quick reaction saved her from falling. Kate caught Angela's eye. For a split second, they were on the same wavelength.

Sorry, she mouthed.

Angela shrugged. *Whatever*.

* * *

Holly leaned forward. Watching Kate ride Magician was awesome but not as awesome as riding him herself. She glanced toward the private box where two women sat with iPads, clipboards, and cell phones. From the red-and-blue logos on their matching navy windbreakers, Holly guessed they were the USEF talent scouts.

The bell rang.

Kate trotted down the centerline, halted, and saluted the judges, who sat in a circular gazebo with a wooden roof and window boxes filled with yellow pansies. More pansies flanked each letter around the arena. Holly crossed her fingers that Magician wouldn't suddenly decide to have a flowery snack.

Trot forward. Turn right at C . . .

Holly knew this routine as well as she knew her own. They'd practiced it together every day since Kate returned to the barn—extended trot across the diagonal, a twenty-meter circle, back to a walk, then transition into a canter.

Would Magician balk at the flying change?

No, her brilliant horse made it look as easy as skipping. Holly relaxed. Just a couple of half passes, another circle, then a working trot, and Kate was home free.

"Sweet," said a voice behind her.

Holly turned. He looked familiar—dark hair, scuffed brown riding boots, great tan. He'd probably been on the winter show circuit in Florida.

"Lockie Malone," he said, smiling.

Of course, Holly thought. *The guy who found Ragtime for Mrs. Dean and then gave a totally awesome clinic at Timber Ridge in January.*

His advice had branded itself on Holly's brain:

A good rider gets a lot out of a horse without taking a lot out of the horse.

"Hi," she said. "I'm Holly Chapman."

"And you've got a great horse," he said, watching Kate halt and give her final bow. "Let me know if you ever want to sell him."

"*Sell him?*" Holly squeaked. She wasn't like Angela, who got a new horse every year. "I've still got my first pony."

"So do I," Lockie Malone said, rubbing his chin. "Well, sort of." Then burst out laughing and pointed over Holly's shoulder. "Oh, my god."

Laughter rippled through the audience as Magician, clearly bored by whatever it was the judges were telling

Kate, had helped himself to a mouthful of pansies. People whipped out cell phones. Lockie snapped a picture.

Kate bowed her head.

With a white-gloved hand, she covered her eyes while Magician happily munched on the pansies, roots dangling from his mouth like brown hair, as if he'd pulled off someone's wig. Holly could imagine how embarrassed Kate felt but couldn't help laughing. This was too funny, too . . .

"Your horse just bought the judges," Lockie said. "*And* the USEF scouts."

Both were tapping madly on their iPads.

Was Mrs. Dean taking notes?

Holly looked at the warm-up ring, but there was no sign of Angela or her mother. Just her own, who blew her a kiss and mouthed, *Love it.*

11

Within twenty minutes, photos of Magician and his colorful snack hit the web. Even *Dressage Today* tweeted about it.

"How can I top that?" Jennifer groaned.

She'd just saddled Rebel and was about to head for the practice ring with Adam.

"Dumb luck?" he quipped.

"No," Holly said, grinning. "Strategy."

Kate hosed off Magician's legs, then put him on the crossties. Holly had already researched pansies and confirmed that they were non-toxic to horses. After this, nobody would remember Magician's flawless flying change, his perfect twenty-meter circles, or their score of sixty-nine percent. From now on, he'd be known as the horse that ate pansies.

"We're two of a kind," Kate whispered, "but you're way cooler than me. I'm just the nobody who blew off Nathan Crane."

* * *

Jennifer and Adam racked up dressage scores in the middle sixties. Angela was nowhere to be found. She'd dumped Ragtime in his stall and disappeared—probably to a five-star hotel, complete with indoor pool, beauty spa, and gourmet dining.

Everyone else had opted for the Horse Park.

Its dormitories offered bunk beds, a cafeteria, and communal bathrooms in two-story buildings clustered around a small quadrangle where early daffodils bloomed hopefully amid old leaves and new mulch.

"This is fabulous," Holly squealed, climbing into her top bunk. She hung her head over the edge like Snoopy peering down from his doghouse. "We're in an Olympic village."

"Minus the superstars," Kate said.

"Wrong," Holly said. "We've got USEF scouts and Lockie Malone."

"Yeah, but he's gone."

Earlier, he'd wished them both good luck and left for his barn in western Connecticut. "Come and visit," he'd said. "Bittersweet Farm in Newbury."

Holly asked Kate, "Is your old barn here?"

"Don't know," she replied.

She hadn't even looked for Sandpiper Stables. She'd been too busy splitting chores with Holly to go traipsing through the other three barns. Pages rustled as Holly thumbed the Festival's glossy catalog.

"They're not listed," she said. "But Northbrook is."

For a moment, Kate couldn't place it. There were dozens of barns and training stables competing at the Festival, some from as far away as Maryland and Pennsylvania.

"Northbrook?" she said.

"City woman," Holly said. "Remember?"

"*Skywalker*," they both said at once.

Shortly before Christmas, a stranger dressed in New York business clothes and high heels had walked into Timber Ridge and bought Angela's old horse for her niece who rode at Northbrook Farm. A week later, Ragtime had shown up in Skywalker's stall, and Angela hadn't learned about the switch until she got home from a ski vacation in Colorado.

"Do you think Skywalker's here?" Kate said.

Holly shrugged. "Let's keep an eye out. Light bay, no white markings. Should be easy to spot, right?"

"Not," Kate said.

Angela's old horse looked almost exactly like her new one. Bays were a dime a dozen—so were browns, dappled grays, and chestnuts. Even Morgans with flaxen manes and tails like Tapestry weren't that rare on the show circuit these days.

Judges didn't pin them often, though.

The big money still preferred Thoroughbreds and European warmbloods—bays, blacks, and elegant dark browns with just the right amount of white. A homely Quarter Horse like Pardner—bald face and mismatched eyes—wouldn't stand a chance in this crowd, even if he could turn on a dime.

That night after Holly went to sleep, Kate pulled out the book Holly had given her for her birthday. She hadn't expected to enjoy it, but she soon found herself totally caught up with the main character, who had Olympic dreams and rode a flashy chestnut that looked exactly like Tapestry.

* * *

Brad arrived at Long River the next morning with Sue and Robin. They'd gotten an early start and had left Aunt Bea and Mr. Evans in charge of the Timber Ridge barn.

"Good timing, dude," Jennifer said.

They were about to leave for the cross-country course. Adam would be up first, followed by Angela. Kate kept watching out for Skywalker, but as she'd pointed out to Holly, bays were all over the place.

"How's it going?" Brad said.

Kate yawned. She'd stayed up way too late reading. "Okay, I guess."

"I saw Magician eat the pansies."

"So did a bazillion others," Kate said. It kept coming back to haunt her, over and over, like the way she'd tossed off Nathan Crane at the premiere. That stupid video was still trending on Twitter and YouTube.

Had Brad seen it?

His voice on her cell phone had come through loud and clear. One of Nathan's fan pages had called him *the mystery guy*. Kate wished, for the millionth time, that she hadn't turned up her speakerphone. It wasn't fair to Brad. She'd used him to get her own back on Nathan.

Brad said, "You'll live it down."

"How about you?"

"No problem."

"I'm sorry," Kate said.

Liz reminded her riders to double-check the course map. "There are two levels of jumps," she said. "Take the lower ones, okay?"

"Why?" Angela said.

"Because you're novices, not experts," Liz said. "Just follow the markers, keep a steady pace, and be conservative. Don't run out of horse before you finish the course."

"Are you saying that my daughter's not an expert?" Mrs. Dean said.

She'd come out of nowhere, the way she always did, wobbling about on outrageously high heels and waving her overdressed arms like a clown. Ragtime tossed his head.

"Yes," Liz said, sounding less than patient. "Angela's a kid with a brilliant horse, but she's—"

The barn's loudspeaker interrupted: "Will riders please . . ."

"Good thing," Holly muttered once the announcement was over and Mrs. Dean had tottered off. "Otherwise Mom would've lost her cool."

Following signposts, they headed for the cross-country course. The warm-up area was filled with novice riders on chestnuts, dappled grays, blacks, and bright bays, but none that looked exactly like Skywalker. Kate was sure she'd recognize him. And if she didn't, surely Angela would.

* * *

Cheered on by Holly, Adam galloped over the finish line. "We went clear," he said, patting Domino's sweaty neck. Liz draped a cooler over his back.

"No time faults, either," she said. "Well done."

"*Mom*," Holly warned. "He's *not* on our team."

"Then stop cheering for him," Kate said.

Holly stuck out her tongue.

Riders left the starting box at three-minute intervals— boom, boom, boom—like clockwork. Hooves pounded and dirt flew as horses galloped toward the first fence.

Then it was Angela's turn.

She nodded while Liz issued final instructions. For once, it looked as if Angela was actually listening, when Mrs. Dean trundled up in a golf cart driven by a show official. Angela's face froze into its familiar mask. She crammed on her helmet.

"Good luck," Kate said.

"Thanks," Angela muttered, then wheeled Ragtime around and cantered off.

"Angela, I—" Mrs. Dean almost fell getting out of the cart.

Liz steadied her. "She needs to focus."

"But—"

Down came the starter's flag and Angela bolted forward. She cleared the first jump, roared down the hill, and was gone from sight in less than a minute.

"If Angela keeps that up," Holly said, "she'll get time faults for going too fast." She ran her hand down Tapestry's loose mane, still curly from its braid. "Don't get any ideas, okay?"

"She won't," Kate said, then watched—heart in her mouth—as Holly took her turn in the starting box. Some of the horses balked and had to be led into it, but Tapestry just flicked her ears as if to say, *Let's go. I've done this before.*

But she hadn't.

This was Tapestry's first real cross-country event, and Kate wasn't riding her. They'd done a hunter pace together last fall, and Holly had schooled Tapestry over the Timber Ridge hunt course, but . . .

Then they were off.

Over the rustic rails, down the hill, and around the first corner. Out of sight. In her mind's eye, Kate ran through the Long River cross-country course: *Red markers on the right; white ones on the left. Jump the lower fences.*

It would be her turn after Jennifer. With luck, they'd be all done by early afternoon.

Kate wiped sweat off her forehead.

She should've worn a t-shirt beneath her body protector, not a hoodie. The temperature had already hit seventy; local news predicted it would be almost eighty tomorrow.

Beach weather.

Warm sand between your bare toes; rock pools teaming with hermit crabs and tiny fish that darted about like quicksilver. Beady-eyed seagulls on the lookout for food, and—

"You ready?" Brad said.

Kate pulled herself together. "I guess."

"How about we hit the beach?"

Had he read her mind?

"Now?"

He grinned. "I think you'd better ride first, huh?"

Kate was about to reply when Holly came galloping

back, face flushed and grinning like a kid with her first ribbon. "Nailed it!" she yelled.

A clear round for Timber Ridge.

Then Jennifer returned with twenty faults—same as Angela—which was awesome, given that most riders in their division had gotten forty faults and more. No wonder Liz was smiling and getting slapped on the back by other trainers. Even though Timber Ridge wasn't an official team this time, the individual performances were really cool for Liz. She'd be in demand for clinics and invited to judge horse shows.

Her reputation would grow.

A slender girl with a blond pigtail that flopped halfway down her back trotted by on a light bay gelding. Was that Skywalker? Kate glanced at Holly, but she was busy cooling off Tapestry and telling Liz how her ride had gone. When Kate looked again, the girl was already out of the starting gate and over the first fence.

Too far away to see properly.

Time to concentrate, get her mind on the job . . . and off Brad Piretti. He gave her a thumbs-up. "Good luck."

Magician slipped easily into the starting gate. Seconds later, they were off. Holly's horse tugged at the bit. He wanted to race, but Kate held him back. With the first jump behind them, they cantered down the slope and turned into the woods. A wide trail opened up, then forked.

Red on the right; white on the left.

Veering right, Kate jumped a low palisade, followed by a line of rubber tires painted in primary colors. Magician didn't even falter.

"Good boy," Kate said.

They leaped over a log pile, then two brush jumps, and tackled an in-and-out with no trouble. The trail spilled into an open meadow, just like the one at the Timber Ridge hunt course. Kate relaxed. This was familiar ground. Ahead was a narrow gate.

Some horses hated narrow jumps.

They ran out or refused.

Kate moved into a half seat. Magician flicked his ears as if to say, *Are you sure about this?* then bounded forward. Over the gate they went.

Clear.

Next came the water. It wasn't deep—hardly more than a large puddle—but it didn't take much to get Magician on his knees and splashing about like a toddler in a wading pool.

"Go, go, go!" Kate yelled.

Her mind shot back to the screen test for *Moonlight*, when Magician had taken an unscheduled dip in front of the film crew's cameras. Kate was supposed to ride Magician down the stream, not swim in it.

But Holly's horse had other ideas.

His legs had folded like the spines of a broken um-

brella, and he'd collapsed happily into the water. Giles
Ballantine had loved it and said it's what had won Kate
the stunt-double role—well, that and riding bareback. But
swimming in a cross-country event wouldn't earn them
any points.

This time, Magician listened.

He plunged into the shallow pond and over the low
crossrails, then out again, scrambling up the bank. Then
came a picnic bench and Magician soared over that as
well.

Was there anything he wouldn't jump?

They cantered on, past the higher fences that the advanced riders would take. Two more jumps and they were
done. One was a ditch; the last was a coop—Tapestry's
nemesis.

Amazingly, she'd jumped it clear with Holly.

Kate crossed her fingers. Ever since last summer when
Tapestry had a serious meltdown over chicken coops,
Kate had avoided them. She tried not to let her anxiety
flow through the reins to Magician's sensitive mouth. He
soldiered up the last hill. Over the ditch—no problem—
and onward to the coop.

The end was in sight.

Warm air brushed Kate's face, just like a mid-summer
day. If she wasn't wearing her helmet, the breeze would be
ruffling her hair and maybe she'd stop to pick a few
daisies. A trip to the beach with Brad sounded like fun.
They'd invite Holly and—

Without warning, Magician slid to a halt. He swerved sideways, and Kate barely managed to keep her seat. She shifted herself back into the saddle, reclaimed her stirrups.

Must. Not. Turn. Around.

That would count as a refusal.

This wasn't Magician's fault. It was hers. She'd been daydreaming, not concentrating. Firmly, Kate put her legs onto Holly's horse and shortened the reins.

Are you listening?

Yes.

"Then let's go," Kate said.

In one stride, Magician frog-jumped the coop as if it were full of chickens about to leap out and squawk. Then they galloped across the finish line, and Holly threw a cooler over her horse's back the moment he stopped.

"How'd it go?"

"Clear, I think."

"What happened?"

"We had a problem at the coop."

Holly hooted. "Magician's not afraid of coops."

"Then I guess it's my fault," Kate said. "I must be scared of chickens."

"Tapestry's brainwashed you," Holly said, laughing. "She went over it fine with me."

12

DESPITE MAGICIAN'S NEAR REFUSAL at the coop, Kate ended up with no time faults and a clear round on the cross-country.

"It's because you didn't turn away," Liz said.

"Magician jumped it from a standstill," Kate said, still in shock. "I couldn't believe it. One minute we were just standing there in front of that stupid coop. The next, we were flying over it. I almost fell off."

Holly sighed. "My horse is a genius. Agree?"

"Yes," Kate said, flinging her arms around Magician's neck. Holly had told her about Lockie Malone's offer. Kate could no more see Holly selling Magician than she could imagine herself selling Tapestry.

But lots of riders did. They sold horses on once they no longer served their purpose. Kate knew that's what you had to do in order to survive in the upper levels of equestrian competition, like at Devon and Rolex Kentucky.

Even here.

The Festival of Horses was a brand-new event and already it had attracted some of the best young riders in New England. Kate didn't expect a ribbon; she didn't expect to be in the top ten or even the top twenty. Just qualifying for this show was a big deal, at least for her. Holly said the USEF scouts had been all over their iPads after Kate's dressage test.

Thanks to Magician's pansies.

As they rode back to the barn, Kate kept an eye open for the blond girl with the long braid, but she didn't see her. Maybe she'd imagined it, but that girl had looked familiar—like she'd seen her once before, a long time ago.

Brad offered to help with chores.

"Thanks, but it's not allowed," Kate said.

"Why?"

"Because we're judged on stable management at this competition," Holly said. "We have to do all our own work, but you can hang out and watch, if you like. It's great entertainment."

"Ta-dah!" Adam struck a pose with his pitchfork. "And now, appearing for the first time at—"

"—Mountain Laurel," Sue carried on, "we have the amazing Barn-Man. Can he fly? No. Can he leap tall buildings in a single stride? Not a chance. But can he muck stalls?"

"*Yes!*" Holly yelled.

The two snotty girls from earlier that morning walked by, mouths agape as Adam leaped onto a tack trunk and flourished his pitchfork. Brad tossed him a broom; Robin produced a muck bucket and turned it upside-down. Adam promptly stuck one foot on it like a big-game hunter.

Laughing, Kate patted Domino's neck. "Don't worry," she whispered. "He'll get over it."

"Never!" Barn-Man declared.

Still giggling, Kate led Magician into his stall. In the one beside it, Holly was rubbing Tapestry down. Across the aisle, Jennifer did the same with Rebel. There was no sign of Angela. Her horse, still muddy from the cross-country course, stood in his stall amid soiled bedding. Ragtime's water bucket, Kate noticed, was almost empty; his blanket had come undone.

Not good.

"Don't even think about it," Holly whispered.

"What?"

"Doing it for her."

Kate hesitated. She hated to see Timber Ridge with a messy stall, even Angela's. It looked bad—bad for all of them, and especially for Liz. Ignoring Holly, Kate took her grooming box into Ragtime's stall. It didn't take long to brush the mud off his legs, fill his water bucket, and fasten his blanket.

Brad handed her a pitchfork. "Is this allowed?"

"I guess," Kate said, shrugging.

She had no idea if it was breaking the rules for one rider to help another. She glanced both ways down the aisle. There was n sign of judges or anyone looking official carrying an iPad or a clipboard.

"So, the beach," Brad said, as Kate dumped Ragtime's manure into a muck bucket. "Are you, like, okay with it?" He paused. "I mean, you don't have to if—"

"I'd love it," Kate said.

She couldn't babysit Magician's stall all day. And who cared if he messed up his shavings or dropped a few wisps of hay on the ground? This was what horses did. They weren't model horses in a plastic stable.

"Good," Brad said. "Holly and Adam are coming, too."

Kate wondered how long it would take Holly to complain that she had nothing to wear.

It was less than five minutes.

"You can borrow my shorts," Kate said, as they raced into their dorm room.

"What about you?" Holly said.

Kate held up a black tankini. "This."

"I should've listened to you," Holly said, struggling out of her breeches.

"Like, when did you *ever*?"

Armed with whatever towels they could find, they joined Brad and Adam in the parking lot. The guys had blankets and a small cooler.

"What's in it?" Holly said.

"A six-pack of soda."

"That's it?"

"We'll get pizza later."

They took off down Route 9 toward the Connecticut shoreline. Kate ignored Brad's GPS that pointed them to the nearest state park and issued her own directions. It was a private beach, but this early in the season no parking attendants and lifeguards were on duty to shunt them away. They kicked off their shoes and raced for the water.

Low tide. Perfect.

"Yikes," Holly said, skidding to a halt the minute her toes hit the frigid surf.

Brad grimaced. "Cold."

"It's April," Kate said, laughing. "What did you expect?"

But the sand was deliciously warm. They spread out their blankets and towels. Adam made an elaborate sand castle with turrets and a moat; Holly added shells, sea glass, and bits of driftwood. Then they wandered off down the beach, holding hands as they clambered over breakwaters and peered into tidal pools like a pair of toddlers.

Lying back, Kate closed her eyes.

Did it get any better than this? Hanging out at the beach with your best friend and a couple of cute guys, knowing you'd just done pretty good in dressage and cross-country?

Lulled by the comforting sound of seagulls and waves, Kate was about to doze off when reality struck.

Show jumping tomorrow.

Rumors about the course had flown thick and fast. Nobody had seen it yet because the jumps were covered with tarps and wouldn't be unveiled until Sunday morning.

"Submarines and sharks," Jennifer predicted.

Holly had pouted. "But no lifeguards."

Something soft brushed against Kate's hand. She didn't move, but Brad did. He rolled toward her and Kate could see herself reflected in his sunglasses. He said, "Is it over?"

"What?"

"You and Nathan."

"Yes," Kate whispered. Then, more firmly, "Yes, definitely."

Nathan Crane was a book—a fairytale like *Moonlight*—that she'd gotten herself caught up in and wouldn't be reading any more of.

* * *

A traffic accident delayed their return to Long River. Brad pulled off the highway and tried for a detour, but it didn't help. Kate was halfway to frantic by the time she ran into Mountain Laurel. They had horses to feed, and nobody else was supposed to do it for them.

But Magician was vacuuming up his last bits of grain, and so was Tapestry. Their hay nets and water buckets were full, their stalls raked clean. Kate tracked down Jennifer.

"Thanks for feeding our horses."

"I didn't," Jennifer said. "I only fed Rebel because I figured you'd be back at any minute."

Robin and Sue hadn't fed the horses either, and Liz was out for dinner with Dad. Earlier that afternoon, he'd texted Kate that he was coming down and would stay over to watch the jumping tomorrow.

"So who did it?" Kate asked Holly as they sat on tack trunks in the aisle, cleaning bridles. There was a pause, then they both spoke at once.

"*Angela?*"

"But why?" Holly said. "She's got the social skills of a sweat scraper."

Biting back a smile, Kate rubbed saddle soap into her braided reins. Finally, she said, "This is going to sound really dumb—like off-the-wall dumb—but I think Angela did it to get back at her mother."

Holly stared at her. "You're right. It's off the wall."

"No, think about it. I did Angela a favor earlier, right?"

"Yeah," Holly said. "So?"

"And now she did one for us."

"She's never done it before," Holly said. "And what's it got to do with her mother?"

"I bet Angela made sure that her mother knew she was doing us a favor, like feeding our horses, just to make Mrs. Dean mad." Holly tried to interrupt, but Kate held up her hand. "Hear me out, okay?"

"Okay."

"Mrs. Dean's really pushing Angela, I mean pushing hard. She wants Angela to win and get noticed by the USEF scouts more than Angela does. But Angela's flubbing up."

"On purpose?" Holy said.

"I don't know, but she's never bonded with Ragtime and now he's unhappy about it."

Holly nodded. "I'll buy that. Go on."

"Angela's being nice to us—well, as nice as she can be—as a way of getting back at her mother."

"Why?"

"For selling Skywalker."

"Oh, get real," Holly said. "When's the last time Angela gave two figs about a horse?"

"You got any other explanation?"

"No, but—"

"There's nobody else who'd feed our horses," Kate said, "unless those two snotty girls did it."

"Yeah, right," Holly said.

Kate finished her bridle. "Let's go exploring."

"Where?"

"The other barns. Come on."

* * *

They cruised through Mark Twain and Nutmeg and were halfway down the Charter Oak aisle when Kate saw her again. "I know that girl. I've seen her before."

"Me, too," Holly said. "This morning, at the—"

"No, before that," Kate said. "Like long ago."

Wearing ear buds and snapping her fingers, the blond girl sat on a folding chair outside a tack stall draped with blue and gold curtains. Through the opening, Kate caught a glimpse of gleaming saddles, spring flowers, and glossy photographs. Rush mats covered the dirt floor.

"So ask her," Holly said. "Go on."

Kate shuffled forward. "Hi."

The girl pulled out her earbuds. She had two braids now, and Kate had a sudden memory of getting in big trouble with Mom at a horse show when—

"Are you Kate?"

"Yes," Kate choked out.

"I'm Emily Nelson," the girl said. "I hit your pony, re-member?"

It all came tumbling back—a 4-H show with Webster, Kate's favorite riding-school pony. He'd gotten loose from the trailer, wandered off, and helped himself to another pony's hay net. The girl with two blond pigtails had hit him.

"And I hit you back," Kate said.

Emily grinned. "I deserved it."

"What's going on?" Holly said.

With Emily's help, Kate explained how they'd cried and apologized, then hung out together, cheering one another on. Kate had won a yellow ribbon in walk-trot; Emily had picked up the blue.

Holly slapped Emily a high five. "Cool."

"So, which farm is this?" Kate said.

There wasn't a sign above the tack stall—just the blue-and-gold drapes which were pretty impressive, almost like theater curtains. They had valances with gold fringe and—

"Northbrook," Emily said. "Come and see my horse."

They followed her down the aisle, past a dozen stalls with blue drapes and matching blue tack trunks lined up so precisely that Kate had visions of secret grooms with measuring tapes at midnight, making sure it was all perfect.

Emily stopped. "Here he is."

"*Skywalker?*" Kate said.

The bay gelding had no star, no white markings. He

wore a cribbing strap around his neck. It had to be Angela's old horse.

"Yes," Emily said. "How did you know?"

"He used to live at our barn," Holly said. "Timber Ridge in Vermont."

"So, who owned him?"

"Angela Dean," Holly replied.

"Is she here?"

Kate nodded. "Her new horse is called Ragtime. He's a light bay and looks just like Skywalker."

"But I bet he's not as good," Emily said, as Skywalker nuzzled her hand. She gave him a hug, then took off his cribbing strap. "He really doesn't need this any more."

"Wow," Holly said, sounding impressed. "That's cool. He used to crib all the time because Angela wouldn't let him go outside."

"Why?"

"She didn't want him to get dirty," Holly said. "She hates grooming and cleaning tack."

Just then, Kate's cell phone rang. She turned away to answer it. "Hello."

"Hi," Brad said. "We've got pizza."

13

Speculation about the jumps shifted into high gear at breakfast on Sunday morning.

"Killer whales," one rider said.

"Pirate ships," said another, "with parrots and a gangplank."

Kate ignored them. As the rumors grew even more outrageous, she quietly finished her scrambled eggs, then went outside to look at the course for herself—and gasped.

"Told you," Jennifer said.

Overnight, beach umbrellas had sprouted like mushrooms. A line of yellow ducks fronted the Liverpool, and two bright-red anchors marked the starting gate. Surfboards and rowboat oars doubled as uprights and wings—a nautical theme gone completely mad.

"Tapestry's gonna freak," Holly moaned.

Glumly, Kate nodded. "So will Magician."

After feeding their horses, they walked the course with Liz, counting strides and figuring the best distance. The jumps weren't high, just really weird, especially the breakwater covered in seaweed and fake barnacles, with a plastic seagull sitting at one end and a model lighthouse at the other.

Angela said, "This is stupid."

For once, Kate agreed with her. Horses weren't water creatures—unless you believed in kelpies.

Adam slapped his forehead. "I knew I'd forgotten something," he said, eyeing the combination jump, a dazzling display of red-and-white rails, beach balls, and two wooden seals.

"What?" Holly said.

"Swim fins and goggles."

* * *

Back at the Mountain Laurel barn, Liz gathered her anxious riders for a pep talk. "They're just jumps," she said. "Your horse won't see a breakwater or lobster pots or canoe paddles. He'll see rails and shapes like he always does, and it's your job to tell him they're nothing to be afraid of."

"Will it be timed?" Jennifer said.

"No," Liz said. "So don't cut corners or rush your fences, okay?"

"What about faults?" Kate said.

The Festival had used its own scoring system for cross-country and dressage. She'd never have gotten a sixty-nine on her freestyle if it had been scored as a regular test—more like the mid-fifties.

"Ten for knockdowns and refusals," Liz said, checking her paperwork. "Three refusals and you're out. Ditto falling off, so glue yourself into that saddle."

"Easy for Mom to say," Holly grumbled as she finished rebraiding Magician's mane. "Shall I do his tail?"

"Thanks," Kate said. "That'd be great."

She'd just seen Angela slip out of Ragtime's stall and wanted to catch her alone. Ever since meeting Emily the night before, Kate couldn't get Skywalker out of her mind. Did Angela know about him? Had it somehow prompted her to feed their horses as a way of punishing her mother?

Holly said Kate's theory was nuts.

But she wanted to make sure. So while Holly was occupied with Magician, Kate quietly followed Angela away from the barn and along winding paths toward the dorms. Angela parked herself on a wooden bench in the quadrangle, then leaned forward and picked a daffodil. She held it to her nose.

For a few seconds, Kate thought Angela was going to cry. Or maybe she was allergic to flowers. Her face was puffy, her eyes red and raw.

"What's wrong?" Kate said.

Angela sniffed. "Nothing."

"Can I sit down?"

"It's a free country."

Cautiously, Kate perched at the end of the bench. It felt really odd to be on her own with Angela, who never traveled without a cheering team—Kristina James or her cousin Courtney. At school, they were inseparable. You never saw one without the other two.

"Where's Kristina?" Kate said.

She hadn't qualified for the Festival, but she was Angela's best friend. Kate figured she'd be here to support Angela, the way Brad, Robin, and Sue had shown up to cheer for all of them.

"With Courtney," Angela said. "On the beach."

"Here?"

"No, stupid. In the Bahamas."

Kate gritted her teeth. It would be so easy—and a lot less stressful—to just get up and leave Angela to figure things out on her own. Instead, Kate said, "Well, anyway. Thank you."

"What for?"

"Feeding my horse," Kate said. "Last night."

"No biggie," Angela said and burst into tears.

Without thinking, Kate shifted closer and put her arm awkwardly around Angela's shoulders, then realized it might not have been the best move. Angela stiffened but didn't push her away.

Was it Mrs. Dean? Had she really gotten to Angela this time? Kate didn't know how to ask. Her experience with mothers was on a totally different planet than Angela's.

Haltingly, she said, "Skywalker's here."

"I know." Angela cried even harder.

Kate opened her mouth, then shut it again. What could she say?

Skywalker's doing great? He doesn't need a cribbing strap any more? He's got a girl who absolutely adores him?

Emily had made that quite clear.

"He's the best horse *ever*," she'd declared just before Kate and Holly left the Charter Oak barn. "We did super in dressage and went clear on the cross-country." Then she'd smothered Angela's old horse with kisses and fed him half a dozen carrots.

Angela had never done that with Skywalker.

She didn't do it with Ragtime, either. She didn't hug him or kiss him or feed him treats the way everyone else did with their horses. She stood back indifferently and got others to take care of him.

Was *that* the problem?

With Angela sobbing quietly beside her, Kate thought it through. Mrs. Dean bought Angela a new horse every year. She never had a chance to bond. Maybe she didn't even dare, because if she fell in love with a horse—with any animal—and it was suddenly yanked away and re-placed with the latest model . . . then what?

She got a broken heart.

"Don't tell anyone," Angela whispered.

"I won't."

"Not even Holly."

"I promise."

For a few precious minutes, they were two girls on the same page. But it wouldn't last. Mrs. Dean would take over, and Angela's mask would slam down like a prison gate. She'd shut out everyone except her superficial friends.

"I had a pony once," Angela said.

Kate waited.

"I taught him to bow and shake hands. He followed me everywhere, without a lead rope," Angela said. "Like a puppy." She caught her breath. "But one day he wasn't in the barn, and—"

"At Timber Ridge?"

"No, the place we lived before."

"Where did he go?" Kate said.

It wasn't hard to imagine Mrs. Dean selling the pony

without telling Angela. No wonder she was scared to fall in love with a horse, with anything.

"I don't know."

"Could you find him?"

Angela wiped her eyes. "Probably, but what's the point? He's better off where he is."

This wasn't the time to argue.

Gently, Kate removed her arm from Angela's shoulders and stood up. "We'd better get back," she said. "We'll be jumping soon."

"Yeah," Angela said, sounding resigned.

* * *

"Where were you?" Holly said. She'd already gotten Magician tacked up and ready to go.

Thinking fast, Kate said, "I needed something . . . from our room."

Luckily, Holly didn't push for details because Kate had no idea what to say next. She was hopeless at lying. She'd tried it once before, when she first came to Timber Ridge, and it almost wrecked her friendship with Holly. But she'd promised Angela to keep quiet.

Liz met them in the collecting ring.

"Jennifer, you're first," she said, "then Adam, so start warming up. Holly, you'll be next, then Angela and Kate."

"All at once?" Holly said. "One after another?"

Her mother smiled. "No, there'll be other riders between you, but it's going pretty fast, so pay attention to the announcer."

"Where's Dad?" Kate said. She'd seen him briefly the previous night, but not this morning.

"On his way," Liz said. "I just texted him."

It still amazed Kate to think of her tech-challenged father using a cell phone and texting. Even more amazing was his newfound love of cooking. Before taking lessons with Liz, he couldn't even boil an egg. Neither could she. The cooking lessons were a Christmas gift from Holly and Kate, encouraged by Aunt Bea, in the hopes of getting their parents together.

It seemed to be working.

But now, Kate's biggest worry was where she and Dad would live once Aunt Marion came home. There wasn't enough room for all of them in the cottage. Dad hadn't said much, but Kate knew he'd been scouring the local paper for another rental. If only they could afford to buy a house, but all Dad's money had gone into the butterfly museum.

"Wake up," Holly said.

"Huh?"

"Emily's in the ring."

Crossing her fingers, Kate watched as Emily and Skywalker cleared fence after fence. Angela's old horse didn't even falter at the beach balls that had already eliminated three other riders.

Had Angela seen this?

Kate couldn't tell, because Mrs. Dean, wearing a navy jacket with more gold braid and brass buttons than an admiral, had claimed Angela's attention and was telling her, loudly, what to do when it was her turn to jump. The loudspeaker hummed into life.

"Our first clear round, folks, for rider one-eighty-seven, Emily Nelson from Northbrook Farm."

"Woot, Emily!" Holly shrieked.

Angela looked up.

No reaction, not even a hint of recognition, but Kate knew Angela had to be hurting inside. Her mother kept prattling on. Mrs. Dean didn't know one end of a horse from another, but she acted as if she knew more than all the horse show judges put together.

Jennifer and Rebel knocked down two rails and got one refusal at the lobster pots.

Thirty faults.

"Not our day," Jennifer said with a rueful grin. "I guess Rebel doesn't like seafood."

Adam went next. Domino refused twice at the break-water and plundered through the Liverpool like a trout fisherman in hip waders.

"Should've worn my swim fins," Adam said.

"No," Holly said, sounding less confident than she had a few minutes before. "Domino should have."

"Hang in there," Kate said. "Tapestry will do fine."

But would she?

Her only issue was with chicken coops. Kate had no idea how Tapestry felt about lobster pots and breakwaters and yellow ducks all in a row. This course was messing up riders left and right. The only clear round, so far, was Emily's. Maybe she'd schooled Skywalker over jumps like this at her barn.

Shortly before lunch, it was Holly's turn.

Nobody else had gotten a clear round, and Kate's heart was in her mouth as Tapestry cantered toward the first fence—a crossrail made from canoe paddles. Over they went, around the lifeguard stand, and toward a vertical panel decorated with red-and-white lifesaving rings—the kind Kate remembered from swimming lessons at the beach.

She held her breath.

Tapestry's hind legs tipped the top rail.

It rocked in its cups, then down it went, taking the panel with it. Goosebumps peppered Kate's arms, and the rest of Holly's round zoomed by in a heart-stopping blur because Kate could barely look. Watching someone else ride your horse over jumps was beyond scary—scarier than doing it yourself.

But Holly was smiling as she left the ring.

"Well done." Liz slapped her boot. "Ten faults."

* * *

They had lunch at Heavenly Hot Dogs. Beneath its green market umbrella, the upscale food cart offered Grey Poupon mustard, designer relish, and ketchup in fancy glass bottles, along with organic sea salt and freshly ground pepper. Even the onions looked different, like they'd been chopped up on TV by a celebrity chef.

"Better than New York?" Kate's father said.

"No," she said, grinning. "But close."

Dad got mustard on his beard yet again, and Liz wiped it off with a napkin, the way she had in Central Park. They smiled at one another as if they shared a secret.

Maybe Dad had found a house to rent.

That would be totally cool and a big load off Kate's mind.

At one o'clock, the jumping resumed. Two riders from Northbrook got forty faults each, and then it was Angela's turn.

"Good luck," Kate said.

But Angela acted as if she hadn't heard. On a tight rein, she aimed Ragtime at the first fence. Over they went, then cleared the life rings, but stopped dead at the lobster pots.

"Not good," Holly muttered.

And it wasn't.

With two more refusals at the beach balls, Angela was eliminated. Stunned into silence, she rode past her enraged mother and headed for the exit gate. It looked, Kate thought, as if Angela wanted to keep on going—out of the horse park, across the fields, and into some other dimension where her mother couldn't follow.

"Kate, get ready," Liz said. "You're up next."

There was no time to feel sorry for Angela, but Kate couldn't help it. Poor Angela. It had to be awful, messing up so badly in front of your teammates and your critical mother. Had she done it on purpose, to punish Mrs. Dean?

The bell rang.

Pulling her scattered wits together, Kate trotted into the ring. From the corner of her eye, she saw the two USEF scouts standing at the rail with their iPads.

Here comes the pansy horse.

No flowers here for Magician to tuck into—just lobsters and beach balls and a hapless seagull, along with two perky seals at jump number seven.

14

KATE FORCED HERSELF TO FOCUS. Despite the oddball jumps, this wasn't the Olympics; it was a regional show in New England. So, okay, the Festival's course designer had gone overboard with his nautical theme, but Magician would be fine as long as nothing flapped.

Last summer they'd ridden past a moving van where two men were unloading a mattress wrapped in yards of flimsy plastic. A breeze had lifted one corner of the plastic and Magician had freaked. He'd almost turned himself inside-out.

But nothing flapped at the paddle crossrails or at the life-ring panel, despite its mock sails, and the lobster pots didn't faze Magician one bit. Big surprise, given they were filled with sparkly starfish and inflatable lobsters. One of Sue's jokes flashed into Kate's mind:

Horses are afraid of only two things—things that move and things that don't.

Ahead were two channel marker buoys. One was painted bright red; the other had a fake bell on top. Kate rode between them, then hung a sharp right past a yellow beach umbrella. Magician gave it a wary eye but didn't break stride.

Time to crank it up.

Emerging from a bank of sand, the breakwater looked totally real. Even the stupid seagull looked real, sitting on a post with its beady eyes aimed toward them. But Magician didn't falter. He leaped over the breakwater, then raced for the Liverpool. Kate kept her legs on him the whole way.

"No swimming," she warned.

A voice from the audience yelled, "That's telling him."

Magician catapulted forward. He soared over the bright blue water, and Kate felt as if she were riding a giant wave—a girl on a dolphin, a surfer dude in Hawaii.

Five jumps behind them; four more to go.

Next up, the combination. Magician's ears swiveled like antennae as they curved around an ice-cream cart with a candy-striped awning. He slowed, veered to one side, and cat-jumped the beach balls at a bad angle. Three choppy strides and over the seals they went, but they didn't have enough impulsion to clear them.

Crack.

Down came a rail.

Aahhh, went the crowd.

To steady herself, Kate grasped one of Magician's knobby little braids. She adjusted her balance, then steered Holly's horse into another right-hand turn toward the green canoe. It lay upside down with a white rail on top. Double-ended paddles—all the colors in a box of crayons—stood to attention on both sides. They jumped clear and Kate felt herself relax.

One more to go—a triple oxer.

It was the only ordinary jump in the course, except its wings looked like display racks at a water sports shop— snorkels, flippers, and boogie boards. All it needed, Kate thought as they approached, were beach chairs and a few artfully arranged bikinis.

Magician lengthened his stride.

"Easy fella," Kate said. "Come back."

But Holly's horse had other ideas. He roared toward the oxer, took off too soon, and launched himself upward like a big black bird. Kate held her breath, waiting for the inevitable crash of falling rails.

But nothing happened.

Somehow, they'd cleared it. Kate heard Holly cheering as they cantered between the finish posts.

"Wow, that was close," Holly said, tossing a cooler over Magician's rump. "What happened?"

"Dunno," Kate said. "Magician just kind of took off."

"Well, you made it," Liz said. "With only ten faults, and that's great. I'm proud of you."

"How about me?" Holly said.

Liz hugged her. "Yes, of course, silly. You, too."

Feeling suddenly overwhelmed, Kate slid off Magician and swapped horses with Holly. Tapestry nuzzled Kate's hand.

"I love you," Kate whispered.

Would things have turned out differently if she'd ridden Tapestry and Holly had ridden her own horse?

Who knew?

Next year, she would have another chance, and she'd be on Tapestry. They'd both be a little older and a lot more experienced. Kate turned to look at the course again. For a few seconds, the jumps blurred and ran together like a watercolor painting left out in the rain. She rubbed her eyes.

Tears?

No, just a piece of grit.

There were no more clear rounds, which put Emily in first place, at least for show jumping. The final results wouldn't be announced for another hour, but Kate didn't think she stood much of a chance at the top ten.

And that was okay.

Far more important was being noticed by the USEF scouts, who'd disappeared into the Northbrook hospitality tent pursued by a determined Mrs. Dean. Would she make excuses for Angela?

Would they even listen?

* * *

While the Timber Ridge kids hung about with their horses, Liz went off to check on Angela, and Kate's dad treated everyone to ice cream. Rebel tried to eat Jennifer's cone. He had a reputation for inhaling vanilla pudding like a vacuum cleaner. The barn's younger kids spoiled him rotten.

"He's a piggy pony," Jennifer said.

Holly grinned. "Me, too."

Devouring her favorite, buttercrunch, she teased Kate for making a mess with the fudge ripple that dribbled down her chin. A drop of chocolate landed on Kate's white ratcatcher. But did it really matter? It wasn't as if she'd get a callback, so who cared if she messed up her shirt?

Riders who hoped for ribbons gathered by the main ring. Trainers paced up and down with cell phones glued to their ears; parents gossiped and looked hopeful.

"Emily's gonna win it," Kate said.

But still the judges demurred. After an interminable

delay, they called ten riders back into the ring. Kate was so focused on Emily and Skywalker that she didn't even recognize her own number.

Holly nudged her.

"That's you," she said, then squealed when her number was called as well.

In a mad rush, they tacked up and mounted their horses.

"My stirrups aren't right," Holly wailed.

Kate grinned. "They're twisted, you nitwit."

She hadn't expected this. Not in a million years. Yes, she'd gone clear on the cross-country, but other riders had beaten her dressage score. Was the written test a game changer? Kate couldn't even remember the questions she'd gotten wrong, never mind the ones she'd gotten right.

And what about stable management?

Had the judges come by yesterday while they were at the beach and faulted Kate for a pile of manure in Magician's stall or penalized Holly because Tapestry's water bucket was half empty? Or had they, thanks to Angela, managed to dodge that bullet?

Breathlessly, Liz raced back.

Ragtime was in his stall, she told them, but there was no sign of Angela.

"She needs her own space right now," Liz said, pulling a cloth from her pocket and wiping mud off Holly's boots. "Well done, you guys. Now, go!"

The moment Holly rode off, Brad kissed the tips of his

fingers and placed them gently on Kate's knee. "For luck," he whispered. "I'd like to do it properly, but I can't reach."

"Hustle," Holly yelled.

Ignoring her, Kate looked at Brad. He was so tall, so unbelievably cute. She wouldn't have to lean far . . .

Was she brave enough to kiss him—and in front of everyone?

Yes . . . no . . .

Yes!

Awkwardly, Kate bent forward, but her stupid helmet got in the way and clonked him on the nose. "Sorry," she said, wanting to shrivel up and die.

Brad gave her a lopsided grin. "It's the thought that I'll remember."

* * *

The ring crew had already removed several jumps, and there was now plenty of space to ride. The judge, wearing a bowler hat and red suspenders, told the stewards to line up the finalists in pairs, and Kate, who'd arrived last found herself beside Holly.

"What's this all about?" she said.

Holly shrugged. "Dunno."

The judge mounted a low stand. "Part of good horsemanship," he said, speaking through his wireless mouthpiece, "is being able to ride someone else's horse. So I want you to swap with your partner."

Kate looked at Holly. "We can't."

"Why not?"

"Because it wouldn't be fair," Kate said. "C'mon."

While the other eight riders dismounted, adjusted stirrups, and exchanged horses, Kate headed for the judge now conferring with his stewards. He glanced at her. "Something wrong?"

"Kind of," Kate said.

Taking turns with Holly, she explained their situation. The judge looked thoughtful for a moment, then said, "So, let me get this straight. You girls are riding each other's horses for this show, right?"

"Yes."

"Okay," he said. "Then I think it's time I saw you ride your own, so would you please switch?"

Kate suppressed a grin. "Yes, sir."

"Right away," Holly added.

With a smile, Kate slid off Magician and took Tapestry's reins. No need to alter stirrups because they both rode at the same length. She hadn't ridden Tapestry in weeks. It felt almost strange to be sitting on her own horse again. From the look on Holly's face, she obviously felt the same way about Magician.

"Hold up," the judge said, looking directly at Kate. "I've seen you before. Didn't you jump at the Hampshire Classic without your stirrups?"

Kate gulped. "Yes."

Her stirrup had flown off at the third fence. She'd

promptly kicked the other one free and wound up riding the course with no stirrups at all. The judge turned toward Holly. "And you, young lady. I seem to remember you were in a wheelchair the last time I saw you."

"That's right," Holly said.

The judge gave a low whistle, then caught his breath and told everyone to circle the arena. "No jumping," he said, waving toward the breakwater, "so don't try to impress me."

It broke the tension.

Emily led off on a dappled gray gelding, followed by a boy on Skywalker. Kate and Holly took up the rear. They walked, then trotted, and finally cantered around the judge. He lined them up again and asked for individual workouts.

"Just canter a simple figure eight, then halt and back up four steps." He nodded at Emily. "You go first."

The gray performed flawlessly, followed by Skywalker and the boy who'd swapped horses with Emily. Neither horse performed a flying change.

But Magician did.

Yet again, he made it look as easy as skipping. Then it was Kate's turn. Tapestry mouthed the bit and dropped her nose. She swung into a collected canter so smooth it was like riding a rocking horse.

Kate's heart did a double bump.

This was *her* horse. She'd rescued her and trained her, and she loved her to pieces. They made a perfect circle, switched leads, and made another. Tapestry halted square and backed up.

One, two, three, four.

Kate nodded at the judge. He tipped his hat.

Beside him stood the two USEF scouts, along with a steward holding a rack of ribbons that reminded Kate of a rainbow. Dad and Liz stood at the rail. Were they holding hands again? Kate couldn't be sure, but she hoped so. Brad and Jennifer had front row seats in the bleachers. Behind them were Sue and Robin.

Even Angela was there, standing outside the Northbrook tent, half hidden in the late afternoon shadows. Kate felt a pang of sympathy. This had to be killing her.

The judge had them switch back to the horses they'd started with. Predictably, Emily and Skywalker took the blue ribbon. No surprise there. Second and third went to riders Kate didn't know from barns in Maryland and Pennsylvania. Fourth place went to another Northbrook rider. The steward held up two more ribbons—one pink, the other green.

Fifth and sixth places.

"It seems we have a tie," the judge said, nodding at Kate and Holly. "But we don't have two pink ribbons."

* * *

Kate and Holly held hands as they cantered side by side around the arena, ribbons fluttering from their horses' bridles—pink for Magician and green for Tapestry.

"We'll share," Holly had told the judge.

Kate grinned. "No problem."

One of the USEF scouts met them at the gate. "Well done," she said. "Do you have a minute?"

Liz joined them. "Of course."

"Your riders show great promise," the woman said to Liz. "So if it's okay with you, we'll be keeping an eye on them."

"In case we get in trouble?" Holly said.

The USEF scout laughed. "I'm sure you'll do that," she said, before leaving. "That's part of growing up."

Growing up . . . moving forward.

Dad said, "Kate, I've got more good news."

"What?"

"Your aunt's staying in South Carolina until July, so we've got the cottage for another three months."

"Whooey!" Holly yelled.

Something inside Kate shifted. The load she'd been carrying just upped and flew away like one of Dad's butterflies. She took off her helmet and tossed it toward Holly.

Brad stepped in and caught it.

"Okay," he said. "*Now* will you kiss me?"

Sign up for our mailing list and be among the first to know when the next Timber Ridge Riders book will be out.

Send your email address to:
timberridgeriders@gmail.com

For more information about the series, visit:
www.timberridgeriders.com

Note: all email addresses are kept strictly confidential

Coming soon . . .
FLYING CHANGES, Book 10 in the
exciting **Timber Ridge Riders** series

Now that summer is here, Kate and Holly are off to Beaumont Park in England to train with Jennifer West's famous Olympic grandmother. It all goes according to plan . . . until a kidnapping makes sensational headlines and drags the girls into an adventure they could never have imagined.

About the Author

MAGGIE DANA'S FIRST RIDING LESSON, at the age of five, was less than wonderful. She hated it so much, she didn't try again for another three years. But all it took was the right horse and the right instructor and she was hooked.

After that, Maggie begged for her own pony and was lucky enough to get one. Smoky was a black New Forest pony who loved to eat vanilla pudding and drink tea, and he became her constant companion. Maggie even rode him to school one day and tethered him to the bicycle rack . . . but not for long because all the other kids wanted pony rides, much to their teachers' dismay.

Maggie and Smoky competed in Pony Club trials and won several ribbons. But mostly, they had fun—trail riding and hanging out with other horse-crazy girls. At horse camp, Maggie and her teammates spent one night sleeping in the barn, except they didn't get much sleep because the horses snored. The next morning, everyone was tired and cranky, especially when told to jump without stirrups.

Born and raised in England, Maggie now makes her home on the Connecticut shoreline. When not mucking stalls or grooming shaggy ponies, Maggie enjoys spending time with her family and writing the next book in her TIMBER RIDGE RIDERS series.

28050443R00111

Made in the USA
Middletown, DE
31 December 2015